Promises to Keep

Also by Patricia Sands

The Bridge Club

The Promise of Provence

Love In Provence ~ Book Two

Promises to Keep

~ A Novel

Patricia Sands

Promises to Keep: A novel
ISBN 978-0-9919313-3-0

Page design and layout by WeMakeBooks.ca
Cover artwork by Scott Collie
Cover design by Carrie Spencer

Prologue

Katherine dropped the small suitcase on the bed and burst into tears. Her heart was aching, but she had no choice. She had to leave this home, this country, and the man she loved. For how long was another question.

After a moment, she wiped her eyes and began selecting what she needed to take with her, but still she wept softly as she folded and packed a few things. She did not need to take much because she was returning to her Toronto home and a closet full of winter clothes. She sat down on the bed for a moment, listening to the strains of smooth jazz drifting down the hallway and wondering why life had dealt this blow, just when things were going so well.

There were two reasons she was leaving. The first she had known for a long time. She had to return to Toronto at some point in order to apply for permission for an extended stay—perhaps the rest of her lifetime—in France. She could apply only from Canada and would have to wait there for the long-stay visa to be issued. While she waited, she would take care of matters there, either selling or renting her house and storing or selling her furniture. Then, once the visa arrived, she would fly back here to Philippe, her love, her partner and the source of her newfound confidence in making these life-changing decisions.

But this was not the reason why she was leaving now. There was a second reason, and it had come out of nowhere and hit her hard.

The lock clicked as she set the combination on her suitcase.

Philippe came quietly into the room, slipping his arms around her from behind.

"I don't want this to happen," he murmured, his breath whispering across her skin as he buried his face in her hair.

1

Two months earlier

One look at Philippe, striding toward her through the terminal, soaked to the skin in his cycling clothes, was all that it took for Katherine to walk away from a scheduled flight back to Toronto. She had been about to pass through security at the international airport in Nice when she heard Philippe call her name. Her usual common sense and caution about unknowns vanished on hearing the voice of the man she loved. She turned around and never looked back.

Outside the terminal, Bernadette, who had driven her to the airport, was already waiting to collect them, with Philippe's bike strapped to the back of her taxi. Once they were seated inside, Philippe confessed that he had phoned Bernadette as she was chauffeuring Katherine to the airport.

"I was on my bike, yelling into my cellphone for her to stall as much as she could. The roads were so wet I almost wiped out a few times. Zut! The only thing that mattered was getting there in time, ma belle," he told her as they clung to each other in the back seat. Katherine felt blissful gathered in his strong arms, oblivious to the mud splattered all over his body.

Soon after she turned the car onto boulevard René Cassin, Bernadette slammed on the brakes, and they lurched forward. "Your luggage! What about eet?" she shouted.

"I completely forgot about it!" Katherine pulled away from Philippe's embrace. "I've got to go back and tell them I'm not taking the flight. They will take the luggage off anyway when I don't show up but I need to tell them."

Bernadette turned the taxi around as soon as she could and drove back to the airport. Philippe took Katherine's hand as he opened the car door and they rushed back into the terminal.

Shaking her head and grinning, Bernadette also got out of the taxi and lit a cigarette.

A half-hour later they were on their way to Antibes. Kat had straightened everything out and arranged for the luggage to be delivered to Philippe's apartment the next day.

A calmer atmosphere prevailed in the back seat, but Katherine's heart was still racing from all the excitement as she and Philippe held hands and leaned into each other, exchanging tender kisses along the way.

In the year since she turned fifty-five, Kat had journeyed from the nadir of what had once been a contented life to a place where she felt strong, independent and able to embrace an entirely new existence. Anger, loss and grief had held her hostage for months, but now love had released the shackles. She was convinced that life was hers for the taking, that she was not too old, that age was no barrier to change and to love.

Bernadette dropped them off at Philippe's apartment. Once inside the vintage elevator cage, which had just enough room for two people who needed no personal space, they reached for each other, and their lips and bodies locked in passion.

After fumbling with the key to the front door, Philippe scooped Katherine into his arms. His dark eyes, intense and glistening, captured hers. Katherine lost herself in them, giving him her body and soul. The heavy door to his apartment slowly swung open.

"They do this in all the American movies, n'est-ce pas?" he said, as he carried her across the threshold, making her feel like a young girl.

She laughed and was surprised at the deep, sexy tone her voice had somehow acquired. Philippe set her down tenderly, rolled her carry-on into the apartment, gently kicked the door shut and drew her back into his embrace.

Covering each other with kisses, they stumbled down the hall to the bedroom, leaving a trail of clothes behind them.

"Welcome home, darling Kat. This is where you belong—chez nous," he said, his lips softly grazing hers, his voice low and throaty.

Waves of love rushed through Katherine.

They toppled onto the bed in a frenzied tangle, letting their urgency take over.

Philippe whispered, "Je t'aime, Katherine. Je t'aime."

"And I love you. Je t'aime," she stuttered, between gasps.

These words, which they previously had held back from saying, they now said over and over throughout a night filled with rapture.

When she woke alone in the morning, Katherine found a single gardenia blossom on the pillow beside her. She knew Philippe had slipped back to see if she was still asleep between collecting the cheeses for his stand at the daily market and opening it at eight o'clock.

She pictured him tiptoeing around the bed like a cat burglar and smiled. Where on earth had he found a gardenia on the last day of October?

She rose, stretching and yawning, infused with a sense of calm about the impulsive decision she had made at the airport. She had never felt this confident during the years she had meekly allowed herself to be guided by her ex-husband, James. Now she knew that the image of protector he had projected had only been a cover for his selfish control of her life.

It had taken intense and raw reflection with a counselor before she was able to face that reality, before she believed that she could change. That, and Philippe's tender love and appreciation of her as a person.

When she arrived in Antibes at the beginning of August, it had not taken long for her to fall in love with the enchanting medieval town that glowed in the warm Mediterranean sun. Falling in love with Philippe had been the surprise. A gift.

She was briefly tempted to head out to her yoga class now, but decided she needed to take things slowly and consider the consequences of her actions.

Once she was up and showered, reality hit her. Was she really doing this? Walking away from everything she'd ever known? Yes, she decided, I am.

Two phone calls were in order. Both her cousin Andrea and her best friend, Molly, would be expecting her to call to say she had arrived back in Toronto.

As usual, Andrea was calm and philosophical. "You've come a long way in a short time," she said. "Don't rush anything, Kat, and do make sure to listen to your heart as well as your head. Take a chance."

"Who knew that the simple home exchange you encouraged me to make would lead to this?" Kat said.

"Who knew? But thank you. I will gladly take credit for it," Andrea laughed. "It's time for you to be happy, to be in love. I'm excited to see how this all plays out. You know Terrence and I liked Philippe immensely from the moment we met him. I never would have expected you to do this, Kat. It's so beautifully out of character. I love it!"

Kat admitted she would have a lot to think about once the fog of love lifted. "Like the job that's been waiting for me. After I call the HR office today, I guess I will be officially unemployed for the first time ever. Eek!"

"I wish you all the happiness in the world," Andrea said, her voice cracking. "Take things one day at a time and the universe will unfold as it should—or something like that."

"I'll keep you posted. Let's keep doing our Monday morning Skype calls. I love you!"

"Me more," Andrea said, as she had their entire lives.

After hanging up, a half-hour passed before Katherine realized she had been sitting the whole time at the kitchen table with her face cradled in her hands.

The euphoria Kat had felt on the phone was fading. Thoughts were swirling through her mind too fast for her to concentrate on any one of them. She realized that her vacation was over, and real life was kicking in. She had just exchanged everything familiar for a life in a country with a language and culture she had yet to learn. How had she reached this place? Routine had ruled her childhood, her education, her career, and, most of all, her marriage.

She shivered and wrapped her arms around herself for comfort.

James. Their twenty-second wedding anniversary. What the hell had made him think that was the right day to leave her?

"It was surprisingly creative behavior, given his pathetic fucking personality," Molly had said, after the fact, when she and Kat had been talking about it. "But, you know, in retrospect, the bastard couldn't have done you a bigger fucking favor."

Kat laughed at the memory of Molly's snarky, expletive-laced comment. The truth of the remark had jolted her at the time, but Molly had been right.

As quickly as the laugh came it went, and her face clouded at the memory of her mother's death just a few months later. She had lived with her mother for a few months after James walked out. In that short time, mother and daughter had connected in a way that only the shared experience of pain and loss can produce.

Kat had gained wisdom and strength from their long conversations as they cooked together and shared meals and countless cups of tea. That time together, the intimacy she felt with her frail mother, was another bonus to the end of her marriage.

The realization that a mother's love for her child rarely ceases had touched her deeply. She felt it whenever her mother took her hand or stroked her arm without thinking, as she had when Kat was young. The memory of that touch now would invariably bring tears to her eyes.

Even though she had always been in close contact with her mother, it wasn't until she moved in with her that she really appreciated what aging and being widowed entails. Her mother had never been one to complain, and Kat had quickly realized how that made it easy for her to overlook how tough it is to be on your own in a body that can no longer do what you want. She learned how much a daily phone call meant to her mom and berated herself for the days she had let her busy life come first. Her mom never said a word about the occasional day she'd missed. It was too late to change that now.

She was about to pick up the phone to call Molly when she decided to see if she was online. The timing was right, and Molly was more fun to talk to on Skype than over the phone. She opened the app and called her number. Molly answered right away, and Kat broke the news that she was staying in France.

"No fuckin' way, Kat!" Molly hollered from Toronto, her startled face lighting up the screen. "You rock! I'm so happy for you—and for Philippe. I expected you to be calling me from here to tell me where to meet up for dinner tonight. I can't believe you had the chutzpah to walk away from your flight."

Molly then went into a long gripe about how this all meant she might not see her best friend for some time.

"I have a feeling it won't be that long, Moll," Kat said. "Bernadette made a few comments on the way back from the airport about visas and stuff. Philippe said he would make some calls this week and see exactly what is needed. I may have to come home to apply to stay longer. Besides I've got to take care of my house."

"Well, you win the fu … er … frickin' Harlequin Romance prize this week in my books, girlfriend. Walking away from your life here to stay with the dude you love. I am so crazy proud of you."

"I have to tell you that I shocked myself. When Philippe showed up at the airport, I couldn't resist. He simply swept me away! It was what I wanted to happen but I wasn't sure enough of myself to admit it until he was standing there, dripping wet."

"Ahhh, just a second. I'm enjoying that image." Molly closed her eyes and grinned. "The one of that swoonworthy body in wet cycling clothes."

Katherine grinned back. "I love being in love."

"Or whatever it's called."

"Well, we actually said the words this time, and it was beautiful. Even though I told you that I didn't care a fig about hearing Philippe say 'I love you,' I was overcome when he did."

"Just proves what I've said before. Passion isn't the private domain of the young and unwrinkled. Enjoy it."

Kat laughed. "I never would have believed it would be in my life now."

Molly's voice softened. "You know I'm happy for you. Thrilled, in fact. Who knew what lay ahead after your asshole husband walked out? Who knew that after all that pain and drama a whole new world would open up for you? This has been such a lesson for me, Katski. Honestly."

"Enough about me, my friend," Kat said, switching from elation to concern. "How are you doing? Is Father DeCarlo still stopping into the Blue Note to catch a set or two of yours on the weekends?"

"Mm-hmm," Molly said, but she quickly changed the subject. "So really, Katski, when do you think you might be back here?"

"Well, I'll definitely have to come back before the one-year anniversary of leaving Toronto. So that would be July sometime."

"I miss you! I can't imagine you living over there for fu … er, for frickin' ever but it sounds like that just might happen."

"Molly, what's going on? It sounds like you're making a concerted effort to tidy up your language."

Molly hooted with laughter in her inimitable way, which always made everyone around her join in. Katherine admired her friend's knack for joy.

Then, in a very proper English accent, Molly said, "You are jolly right. I've been getting counseling, and that's part of the program. No more dropping f-bombs all over the place. Imagine!"

Kat laughed. "I think I might miss it. It's so much a part of you."

"The counselor says my swearing is all tied in to anxiety. It's almost like an addiction, if you can get your head around that idea."

"Well, the change is noticeable."

"It's not so easy to stop."

Kat offered some words of encouragement and then added, " If I end up staying in France, you must promise to visit me here again next summer."

"Damn straight! I'm going to set up a special bank account tomorrow. I'd love to come back."

They chatted about Molly's teaching and singing and her life in general and Katherine was sure she detected a note of optimism, unusual for the Molly she knew. She hoped she was right and made a mental note to ask about it sometime soon. Now she was too wrapped up in her own new life.

The conversation ended quickly after Kat heard Molly's doorbell ring.

"Whoops, that's my next piano lesson arriving. Gotta go. Love you, and I'm seriously so excited for you."

"Me too, Moll. Talk soon."

2

In the following days, Kat and Philippe began to slip into their own routines, but with the awareness that they were now building a life together.

A colorful bouquet of fragrant lilies was delivered to the apartment with a thoughtful note from Philippe's daughter, Adorée, expressing her pleasure at the turn of events and thanking Katherine for bringing happiness back into her father's life. Katherine had met the twenty-three-year-old beauty at the grape harvest weekend at Joy's in September where Philippe had made certain they spent time together.

As he had done for almost twenty years, Philippe left before dawn for the covered market, where he and Gilles, his long-time friend and assistant, set up his popular cheese stand. Now there was a spring to his step that had been missing for many years.

They rolled out the glass-fronted counters and filled them with delicious and aromatic cheeses from all parts of France. Only the finest products would do and Philippe had spent years studying and apprenticing to acquire his well-earned reputation.

Where Philippe was quietly passionate about the cheese they sold, Gilles was flamboyant and engaging. When lineups at their stall grew long with customers wanting Philippe's opinion and suggestions, Gilles would work the queue and take care of simple requests so everyone remained in good humor.

Kat entertained the thought of introducing Gilles to Molly the next time she visited. His hearty laughter sounded like just the right fit for hers—and he was single.

Katherine's days began with yoga and a walk or bike ride. Cycling alone made her feel free and at peace with the world. As much as she loved the weekly rides with Philippe and their local cycling club, she found going alone on secondary roads, away from traffic, both more exhilarating and calming.

The first time she rode alone this week, she remembered how after James left her, she vowed never to cycle again. The memories of their shared involvement in the sport were excruciating in those early days of painful disbelief.

The home exchange in Sainte Mathilde had cured her of that, when her quickest response to a sudden emergency had been to hop on a bike to get help. After leaping that hurdle, cycling through the peaceful countryside of the Luberon reawakened the euphoria she had known on a bike since childhood.

She had returned to Toronto, after that exchange, with renewed commitment to the sport and to not allowing the hurt James had inflicted to rob her of anything good in life.

Now she pedaled on, banishing those thoughts. Her new life seemed all good and cycling was once again a vital part of who she was.

But since shortly after her arrival in Antibes back in the summer, she realized what she loved even more here was simply walking, quietly observing everything around her. It occurred to her that she had traded her early morning Toronto habit of checking all the news services for the early morning delight of watching the old town waking up.

This habit continued now as she spent the early hours strolling the ancient streets and alleyways at the heart of Antibes. As she took in how the light was falling on the cobblestones and the vine-covered houses, she wondered if its beauty would ever become commonplace to her. She took great pleasure in watching the town's cats and dogs join the early line-ups for baguettes; in hearing voices laughing, cajoling; in the sound of chairs scraping and dishes rattling as cafés were set up; in smelling the night's catch from the fishing boats as it was laid out on display down at the quay. She reveled in all of it.

Her camera, not her computer, was now her constant companion. Her focus was on the small world around her, not the bigger picture. She realized she was a news junkie no more and that had to be a good thing.

On the first day of her new life with Philippe, she began a photo journal, an idea that came to her during her morning walk. She set up a separate album on her computer, adding one shot each day, accompanied by a few words: her private gratitude journal.

When she went through that album later, Katherine saw there was a pattern among the photos she'd chosen. She was, to use a phrase she had adopted during her divorce counseling, "redefining the possible."

At some point during her morning walk or ride, she would sit by the sea. The Mediterranean had called to her since she first set eyes on it thirty years earlier. La Grande Bleue, Philippe called it. There was something about the calls of seabirds, about the colors of the sea, the movement of the water, the play of light on the waves that seemed to symbolize the change in herself.

Breathing in the salty air, she considered how her story was changing.

Early on in her counseling, after James left, she struggled with uncertainty and identity. Now she was forging a new path and feeling more confident about who she was and, more importantly, who she wanted to be.

The future had disappeared into a black hole the fateful afternoon of la Katastrophe, as Molly christened it. Now bright with promise and different in every way imaginable, there was a plan developing. Dreams. She was sure there would be stumbling blocks along the way, as there always are, but she felt prepared to face them.

There was no denying the moments of melancholic home sickness that overcame her from time to time. Memories were triggered by something as simple as a smell, a taste or even a color. But those remembrances that brought sadness or a desire for what she once knew as home, often morphed into a reminder of good things that would stay with her no matter where life took her.

At times, in private, she even shed a few tears but came to recognize they were not so much tears of sadness but rather a way of clearing emotional hurdles to bring her back to the reality she had chosen. She had left many anchor points behind, but their absence had opened the door for her to move forward.

It's not that she was completely different; it's that everything around her had altered and she was opening up and embracing that change, taking a chance. And it felt right. Who knew? She smiled at that. She'd been asking herself that same question repeatedly.

"Who knew?" she said out loud now, as she tossed some pebbles into the sea and got to her feet.

She was growing aware of how right Philippe had been when he'd warned her that word of their living together would quickly spread through the old town. Even Monsieur Bouchard, the curmudgeonly owner of the tabac where she purchased a copy of Nice-Matin, the local newspaper, each morning, seemed to be casting his vote. Now when she entered the tiny shop, its walls coated with international papers and tawdry tabloids, he solemnly waved a copy waiting for her by his cash register. At times he showed a hint of a smile and she felt that she had passed inspection.

Usually, after collecting the newspaper, her next move was to sit at a small table by the window in the café, Le Vieil Antibes. After ordering a pot of thé au citron, she would watch the village activity and read the latest news with her dictionary close at hand. "My morning French lesson," she called it.

She ran into Bernadette a couple of times and had coffee with her. With her wild, frizzy, gray hair and tall, slender frame, Katherine's favorite taxi driver and hilarious social commentator, was easy to spot when she rushed through the town on any number of seemingly endless tasks. Her age was indeterminate, her energy limitless, and her knowledge of local affairs without compare. Bernadette herself preferred Swedish men, but still she told Kat that Philippe was "le meilleur homme du pays," the best man in the country, adding with a snort, "even if he is French."

If Kat had no other plan, she would end up at the market with an espresso for Philippe and, for herself, a café au lait, which she was learning to enjoy. She would leave quickly if he was busy, but on slow days, she would sit by the stall for a while as he worked.

Her knees weakened every time she saw him, his handsome face framed by dark brown hair that was a little on the long side and combed back until the ends escaped in small untamed curls. He gives me schoolgirl moments, she thought as her heart fluttered at the very notion of him. She could feel her cheeks flush with desire when their gaze connected with others watching. Who knew I would have those feelings again at this point in life? Who knew?

After returning the cups to the café, she would wander the market, looking for ingredients for dinner if she hadn't already bought fish at the quay.

On Wednesday, she rejoined the expat group in Nice for their weekly "walks and talks." The women welcomed her back warmly, although they were surprised as they thought she had left France for good. Katherine sheepishly laughed and said, "So did I."

She told Philippe she was also going to rejoin her Monday bridge group, at some point.

"I might learn to play bridge with you after the holidays," Philippe responded.

"Is that you or the wine talking?" Kat asked. "I would love it if you did."

She felt a shift in her thinking. She was definitely no longer in vacation mode.

But there were moments, few and far between, when she worried that their love would not last long, and she admitted this to him.

"Moi aussi," Philippe said, "de temps en temps. C'est normal."

Katherine nodded, "We both have fears to conquer, trust to build."

The death of Philippe's wife several years earlier had left him afraid of loving deeply and losing that love again. He told Kat, "You are the first, since Geneviève died, and you make me feel willing to take the risk. I just have to believe we will love each other forever."

Kat struggled to control her tears, but eventually managed to say, "Grief is so powerful. I can only imagine how painful your loss was. Geneviève will always live in your heart, and that's the way it should be."

"Oui"—he stumbled over the first few words—"there ... there are things I must tell you, but not today. Most important is that I now know that I can love again. I thought that was impossible."

They leaned into each other and kissed. The softness of his lips stirred her to her core. "Je t'aime, Katherine. I love you and I love hearing myself say it."

Kat's eyes glistened as she ran her finger lightly down his cheek and across his mouth. "Je t'aime aussi."

She wondered briefly what was troubling him that he couldn't tell her and made a note to bring it up soon. Not today.

"But you have been touched by grief too," Philippe said. "That's part of what makes us strong together."

"D'accord," she whispered. "True."

As much as she didn't want to say it out loud, she found herself admitting that she was worried about their age difference—at forty-six, he was ten years younger than she—and that, at some point, he would be attracted to someone younger.

Philippe laid two fingers on her lips. "Shhh. Don't ever think about that again. There comes a point when age is just a number, and we are both past that. You are strong and beautiful to me, inside and out. That's what counts."

Philippe took her hands and pulled her up from the couch. "Enough talk! Let's go and see what today's catch is at Le Vauban and have a glass of champagne to toast our future."

As they went out the door, he tapped her shoulder. "If it makes you feel any better, everyone thinks I am older than you. You know how the town loves to gossip."

Kat found that adjusting to Philippe's elegant, spacious apartment was a process. It had a completely different feel than either the rustic farmhouse in the Luberon or the cozy fisherman's cottage in the old town, the places she had called home during her exchange visits.

It also did not have one truly comfortable place to sit, except at the kitchen table. Even the couch was hard.

When Kat asked Philippe which was his favorite armchair, he raised an eyebrow. "Aucun," he said. "Not one of them. These are all very old, mostly from my grandparents' house, but we never spent much time sitting around. When we were home there were things to be done, usually in the kitchen, and so we gathered there. Otherwise our social life was outdoors."

She nodded, reminded that she had not missed television for the three months of her exchange and that they rarely turned it on now.

Philippe encouraged her to make the space hers as well, but Kat was all too aware that he had a history in this apartment, and it did not include her. It made her nervous to change much, but she tried.

"I like it when you move the furniture around and make a new look for us. We are beginning our story together." He grinned. "And we will buy some new armchairs, comfortable ones."

Kat eventually pinned her problem down to the fact that nothing in the apartment was hers. Nothing was familiar or gave her the pleasure that comes from carefully chosen pieces of furniture, works of art, or even a simple decoration.

They talked about her sending a shipment from her house, and there was no question the first item to go in the container would be her mother's treasured carpet. There wasn't a great deal else she wanted to ship, but the few other pieces on her list also carried a wealth of meaning for her. It would be good to have them in her new home.

The crammed bookshelves in both the living room and bedroom helped to reveal this man who had captured her heart. Classic novels by Dumas, Hugo and Zola were jammed side by side with what he called the "crazy years"—books by Hemingway, Fitzgerald, and Stein—there was an extensive collection of existentialist works—Camus,

Kierkegaard, Simone de Beauvoir and Sartre—and the more recent works of Paulo Coelho and a writer she had not heard of before, Cees Nooteboom.

"Some of those volumes have come down through several generations," Philippe told her one evening, as she looked through the shelves for another to read, "and I've devoured most of them. The first few years after Geneviève died, I was like a hermit when I was not at the market. I went to a very dark place for quite a while. Reading helped me to survive."

Kat had taken his hand, encouraging him to go on, but he had asked her to give him more time. She could only imagine how much pain comes from watching your beloved spouse slowly die.

Philippe was delighted to discover their shared love of reading, and he teased her with quotes from Sartre once he found out he had been one of her favorite writers in her university years.

"He kept me company in that dark place I mentioned."

Katherine nodded. "Who better?"

After a few days, Kat grew uncomfortable that Philippe was paying most of their expenses. They had not yet talked about finances in any detail, and she thought they should. When she decided she couldn't put the subject off any longer, she said, "I feel awkward bringing it up. But we've never even touched on how I can contribute financially to our life together."

Philippe waved his hand. "It's not important."

"But I feel troubled by it. We should make a plan."

Then she felt she'd been pushy to mention it. The last thing she wanted was for him to think she was pressing for a commitment, and she chided herself inwardly.

Her career had consumed a good part of her life, and she had paid more than half their living expenses during her marriage, so she was amazed to find that she was content not to be working. For now, her small inheritance from her mother was enough to cover her personal expenses, so she still did not have to touch her investments. But she knew that, sooner or later, she'd want her own income and to contribute her share to their life together.

Philippe listened intently as she explained this to him.

"I understand, Kat, but we still have much to decide. You told me, 'One day at a time,' oui? When I talk about our future, you only let me go so far."

"You're right," she agreed, feeling a bit guilty. "On the one hand I want to think long term and on the other, I can't quite go there yet. One day at a time it is, for now."

"D'accord, mon petit minou," he replied, giving her a sly look.

"Pardon? What did you call me?"

"Mon petit minou. In English, your nickname is Kat. Un petit minou is a small cat. That's my nickname for you. Minou."

Kat laughed. That was something else she loved about her life with Philippe: they laughed a lot. "D'accord ... mon petit chou. Mon chouchou! I read that in one of my French exercise books. It rhymes. If I am your petit minou, you will be mon chouchou."

As part of their daily routine, Philippe would arrive with lunch carefully chosen from the day's tempting market products. They planned in advance whether to eat at home or at the rundown family villa he'd inherited, which they hoped to rescue from decades of abandonment, on the Cap d'Antibes. They continued to spend hours clearing and pruning the gardens, as they had begun in October, weeks before he brought Kat back from the airport. Philippe now arranged with a stonemason to begin the restoration of the crumbling stone walls, and they felt excited about moving forward with the dream of opening a small inn.

When he had first taken her there during her home exchange, Katherine had fallen under the spell of this peninsula, which jutted into the sea between the Baie de Cannes and the Baie des Anges. The properties were a mix of large estates, many of them foreign-owned, and small farm plots, like Philippe's, that had managed to elude hungry developers. The hilly woodland at the southern end of the Cap was crossed with small lanes leading nowhere except to a breathtaking view.

Since then, they had biked the peninsula often and hiked the rocky trail along the coast, with a picnic, as Philippe took her to all the special places of his childhood adventures. His deep connections to the area and to his family property were clear.

During the three months she had been on her exchange in Antibes, Katherine would often walk, camera in hand, through the forest and up the chemin du Calvaire, past the twelve stations of the cross that were in various states of disarray. The lighthouse at the summit marked the highest point on the Cap. Each time, she would capture the panoramic view in a different weather and light, and some of these photos made it into her photo journal now. She found herself drawn to the simple small church there, Notre-Dame de la Garoupe. A holy site since the fifth century, votive candles and touching handwritten notes and drawings by sailors, fishermen or their families, covered the walls, watched over by the gilded statue of Notre-Dame de Bon Port. Kat was moved, sometimes to tears, by the powerful intimacy of the pain or gratitude pinned there for all to see.

"Protect, we pray thee, our sailors from the perils of the sea; in the hours of watching, strengthen and sustain them; and grant that in dangers often, in weariness often, they may serve thee with a quiet mind."

And so Katherine spent those early days now, after making her surprising decision to stay with Philippe. Each day seemed to bring them closer, and each morning promised her a new adventure.

3

Minou! If you aren't busy, come up into the hills with me! You're going to want to see this!" Philippe called, as he burst into the apartment at noon. "We haven't explored a new village for a while and I promise you will love this one. But then you love them all, don't you?"

Katherine was editing photos on her computer and looked up in surprise.

"Je suis pressé," Philippe said as he rushed about. "I have to pick up a special order that I'll tell you about in the car. And we'll need warm coats. It will be cooler up there."

"I'm ready!" she said, picking up her camera. Philippe fetched jackets for them from the closet.

He gave her a playful pat as they left the apartment. "No time to wait for the ascenseur. Allez zou! This will be our one week anniversary adventure!" They hurried down the stairs, and Kat laughed at the spontaneity. It was hard to believe only seven days had passed since he carried her over the threshold.

In the walled courtyard where he had parked, Philippe held the car door open for her. It was a courtesy that seemed to be second nature to him, and Kat appreciated it every time. Then he went to unlock the gate. On his way back to the car, he paused and plucked a folded paper from behind the wiper on the driver's side. His jaw tightened and he quickly looked around the courtyard. He scrunched the paper and shoved it into the pocket of his jeans before sliding heavily into his seat. Kat had never seen him angry before.

"What was that?" she asked.

"Rien du tout. Nothing, nothing at all," he answered abruptly.

Putting her hand on his arm, Katherine repeated her question. "I saw the look on your face. It looked like it was something, not nothing."

Philippe exhaled loudly before he covered her hand with his and lifted it to his lips. "Sorry, Minou. It's nothing to worry about, and I'm sorry I spoke so sharply."

"But—"

He squeezed her hand, but he looked pained and his voice had an unfamiliar edge to it. "Seriously, we don't need to talk about it. It's just some business from a long time ago that I thought was finished ..."

A hush hung in the air. Then Philippe started the engine and they drove off.

Torn between wanting to know what was bothering him but not wanting to push, Katherine stayed quiet as Philippe navigated the town's narrow streets and drove them into the countryside.

She had learned years earlier, after being scolded and humiliated by James, that she needed to stay out of some matters. Her throat tightened at the memory. His verbal attacks had felt physical, like a kick in the stomach, and completely foreign to her. She had not experienced or witnessed anything like it before she married him. It had crushed her.

Now she struggled to banish those painful memories. She looked straight ahead, taking some deep breaths but saying nothing, until she knew exactly what it was she wanted to say.

She turned to Philippe and touched his cheek lightly. "You know I'm here if you want to talk about it."

He nodded, staring intently at the road. "Frankly, I hope we never have to talk about it. It's something that should not be part of our life together. I'm sorry you saw this."

After a moment, he glanced at her and tried to smile. "I will make it go away, I promise."

At first the road they were on was flat and uninteresting as it followed the dry, pebbled bed of the Var River. When they turned away from the coast, they could see heavy clouds were gathering in the distance, darkening the sky, and soon they were climbing out of the coastal plain into the hills and the threat of rain. She tried to quell her unease, telling herself, they would work through this, whatever it is. Besides, she thought, it was about time she saw another side to him. No one's perfect.

When Philippe spoke again, his voice had returned to normal. "Let me tell you where we are going this afternoon. You and your camera are going to be very happy."

He started to tell her the history of Entrevaux, the hill town that was their destination, and the tension between them slowly dissipated as they drove onward. The river had disappeared into a gorge below the road, which passed through rugged rock cuts at times. A strong wind jostled the car.

Kat tried to keep the conversation light, unaware that Philippe was keeping a close watch on the rearview mirror. "It's a completely different type of drive from our usual routes in the arrière pays," she said. "The terrain is severe, almost harsh, with all the jagged rock. It feels closed in and mysterious. Where are those expansive views I'm so accustomed to?"

"They will come, but they will be different. It's definitely a complete change as we head into a more Alpine setting."

"And yet we're still so near to the coast."

Just as he was on his motorcycle, Philippe was a fast but safe driver with a feel for how best to manoeuver the car along a challenging route. Today, she was certain he had stepped it up a touch.

"We're now getting into the foothills of the Alps," he said. "It's only an hour's drive to Entrevaux but it feels like a leap five hundred years back in time when the town appears. I have to meet Jacques. He was bringing me ten kilos of his exquisite chèvre. It consistently wins first prize in Alpes Maritimes competitions, by the way. Wait until you taste it."

Kat smiled to see him become his usual enthusiastic self as he spoke about a special cheese.

"His mother lives in Entrevaux and he stopped in to see her. Now his truck won't start, so I said I would meet him there."

The road was now taking them past isolated and semi-abandoned villages hanging off ledges, forsaken by younger generations eager to search for new opportunities.

Using a fast shutter setting, Kat shot photos through the windshield or through the open window. The rain was holding off, and two or three times, she asked him to pull over so she could capture a specific image. She would focus her camera on a striking visual that spoke to her emotionally and withdraw into herself until she knew the image was right. Then she clicked the shutter and reconnected with the world.

"Some of these dwellings appear eerie," she said when they had stopped for her to get out of the car and photograph a cluster of centuries-old buildings clinging precariously to a rocky ledge but surprisingly still occupied. "They're sad, but intriguing. Clumped together the way they are, each tiny community is its own work of art. They're really sculptures in stone, tile and wood. I want to learn their stories."

"I like to watch you do this," he said.

"And I like that you like that," she said as she replaced the lens cap.

Philippe took her hand and pulled her to him. She buried her face in his neck and breathed in the strong, clean smell of him that she loved and that was becoming so familiar.

Peace. This gives me such peace, she realized.

"I love you so much, so very much, and I will never let anything harm what we share. Please trust me," Philippe whispered.

Katherine's eyes searched his face, finally meeting his, before she nodded. When he spoke to her of his love, she was sure that she was the center of his universe.

"I do trust you. That's important to me. What could possibly harm us?"

His arms tightened around her. "Nothing. I will make certain of that."

They stood for a few minutes, just holding each other, their powerful emotions binding them, before resuming the drive. The silence between them was comfortable now.

Here and there, hikers climbing the high, narrow paths on the hillsides above them unexpectedly emerged from the forest. Walking sticks appeared mandatory. Katherine willed her thoughts to focus on these hiking trails and speculate where they might lead and not think about what the mysterious problem Philippe had might be.

Railway tracks paralleled the road, crossing it from time to time, and once they had had to stop at a crossing to let a long freight train through. For some time, the train kept pace with them but now it disappeared into a tunnel, and they began to navigate sharp switchbacks as the road zigzagged upward.

Katherine was jolted out of her thoughts by Philippe swearing loudly and accelerating. His phone began to ring.

"Hold on! Don't turn around!" he ordered. The fierceness of his voice shocked her.

She looked into her side-view mirror and saw a black SUV hard on their tail. The two vehicles screeched through a hairpin turn. Her heart thumping, Kat clutched her armrests, thankful there had been no traffic coming the other way. Thankful, too, that the road was dry.

"Turn my cellphone off," Philippe growled, tossing it in her lap. Stunned by all that was happening, Katherine gripped the deadened phone and stared at it. The sudden stress and the blur of the trees as they passed was frightening.

The chase continued through several more hairpin bends as the road switchbacked down the other side of the mountain spur. Philippe's smaller and sleeker Citroën pulled marginally ahead.

Her pulse still racing, Kat was shocked to hear railroad signals clanging. She looked up to see the barriers ahead begin to lower and the train emerging from the tunnel a short distance away from where the tracks crossed the road.

Philippe's swearing was feverish, and she could understand only a few words.

"What's going on? Who's behind us?"

"Put your head down and close your eyes," he shouted, roughly pulling her down in the seat.

Katherine's last glimpse of the oncoming train made her scream, and she clamped her eyes shut. She realized precisely the risk he was taking. Swerving sharply one way and then the other, the car shuddered and bumped as Philippe raced it across the tracks. The clanging was briefly deafening and a loud scrape could only be the barrier hitting the car roof.

Kat could just hear the squeal of tires on the other side of the train above the rumble of steel wheels on the track.

Back on the smooth road again, Philippe slowed the car and took her hand.

"Oh Christ, Kat! Désolé! Désolé! Are you okay?" he panted, out of breath.

Katherine sat in speechless disbelief, all synapses firing, before howling, "What the hell happened? I can't believe you just did that! Who was chasing us? Why?"

Philippe glanced at her, his eyes full of apology. "I can't believe I did it either. I'm sorry. It was sheer reflex."

He shook his head slowly, still gripping the steering wheel tightly. "I'm not sure who was in that SUV," he said, "but there's no doubt they are connected to a very bad part of my life. A part I have not shared with you."

Katherine stared at him. "That note this morning?"

"It was a warning. I'm so sorry. I didn't think for a minute that anything would happen so soon. I think it was not by chance that they saw us leave and followed us—a scare tactic."

"They? Scare tactic? What are you talking about?"

"I can't pull over. We have to keep going. They may still be after us. Let's leave it alone now and I will tell you the whole story when we get back home. We are expected in Entrevaux and I will need time to tell you everything. Can you accept that?"

"Are we going to be safe?"

"We will be there in a few minutes, and I know where I can hide the car. If they keep coming, they will think I was going higher into the hills to one of the cheese producers. Entrevaux will not be on their radar, I assure you."

"Just tell me we are safe now."

"We are. I promise."

They drove higher, ascending another spur, and then rounding a sharp curve. Suddenly, there it was: a jumble of tiled rooftops stacked up a steep, rocky hillside, overlooked by a dramatic fortification much higher up. The faded browns and grays of structures and nature blended into one.

Kat gasped, in spite of herself and the fright she was still overcoming. "It's like something out of Disney."

The gorge at the edge of the road had deepened, and the river was flowing strongly here, filled by mountain tributaries. Nature had provided a defensible, angled cliff overlooking the steep gorge, and humans had taken advantage of the site.

Philippe turned the car sharply off the road and drove up an embankment to a small parking area across the gorge from the medieval village. He parked the car between two large trucks. From here they had a clear view of the road below through a small break in the trees, but their car would be difficult to spot by anyone driving past.

They unbuckled their seat belts and fell into each other's arms.

"Mon Dieu! I'm so, so sorry for scaring you like that. I'm sorry I yelled."

"I've never been so terrified. I couldn't believe it was happening."

"Moi non plus. I couldn't either."

After a minute, they pulled apart.

"What the hell, Philippe? I mean, what the ...? I've never seen or heard you so angry."

He spoke softly, watching the road. "I've started to tell you this part of my story a few times, but it is hard for me to speak about it. You have brought me such happiness, such a new lease on life, I didn't want anything to spoil it. I never imagined that what is happening now would ever happen."

"Surely, it can't be so bad it would change our feelings for each other?"

He sat quietly for a moment, tapping the dashboard. "This has to do with events that happened when Geneviève was dying. It's complicated. It's serious. And now it has come back to haunt me. I'm afraid you may not want to stay with me when you know about it. You may not be able to."

Katherine waited for him to go on, unsure whether she felt more frightened or confused, and worried that it was their relationship rather than her safety that was in peril.

They both leaned forward when they spotted a black SUV, with tinted windows, racing up the road. Kat was holding her camera and fired off a few quick shots before it disappeared beyond the town. "Maybe we'll be able to read the license plate."

"Your reflexes are unbelievable. Good move!"

"If we get the plate number, we can inform the police."

Philippe frowned. "No police," he said. "What I am asking is unfair, but can you wait just a little longer? I need to sort out some things and then I will tell you the story, the whole sordid story."

Kat hesitated, dire thoughts swirling through her mind. "If you need time for—whatever—of course. But promise me it won't be much longer. You have me frightened and I don't know why. How can you tell me I may need to leave you?"

Philippe held her face gently. "I know I am asking a lot of you. Your patience amazes me. That was my fear talking. I'm sorry I said it. This is not about us but it's something I must fix. Above all, don't doubt this, jamais, I love you."

His voice was so full of emotion, Katherine was reassured.

"Let's go meet Jacques," he said, opening the car door. "With luck, he will have a strong drink to offer us."

A short walk took them to a different world. A stone gatehouse guarded a bridge that crossed the gorge, and they stopped there to read a tiled mosaic plaque. Philippe translated it.

"In 1536, the village was overtaken by the troops of Charles V, the Holy Roman Emperor, after the villagers were betrayed by the ruling duke. Half the population was slaughtered, but the survivors revolted, slashing the throat of the duke and offering the village to the French king, François Ier. In return, François made Entrevaux a royal town and exempted the citizens from taxation, which allowed it to thrive until the Revolution. The cathedral was built in the 1600s and it will surprise you."

They crossed the stone bridge and walked into the village under a portcullis that was flanked by twin fairy-tale towers.

"What a dramatic arrival, and I'm not talking about our car chase." Kat said, raising her camera and firing off shot after shot.

"I can't believe you just joked about that," Philippe said.

"Neither can I." she said.

The narrow alley that sloped up from the bridge opened into a small square, where a fountain spouted cold water from an alpine stream. The crystal clear water streamed through the open lips of two beautifully carved stone faces into the basin below. Philippe leaned in for a drink. "Try it, Minou. You'll taste the difference."

It was so cold it hurt her teeth. But it was delicious.

They were standing in front of the mairie, and a sun dial on its wall indicated it was just after 2:30.

"If we had arrived a little earlier, we could have had lunch there." Philippe pointed to a cozy auberge that was obviously closed. "Are you famished or should we go across to the boulangerie? I didn't plan this well."

"It wasn't planned, period. Besides I seem to have lost my appetite."

The maze of passageways leading off the square was dark and cramped by tall buildings. Oddly placed and steeply angled flights of stone steps were unlike anything Kat had seen before.

"This village has a unique character. The ones in the Luberon and on the coast are delightful, but this one is mysterious. It intrigues me."

The dull light and gusting wind contributed to the village's mystery as they explored it further, Kat's camera shutter working non-stop. Concentrating on composing the images she wanted to capture was helping to take her thoughts off the drive.

Around the next corner, a stooped, petite, elderly woman was slowly sweeping leaves and dust, seemingly in a never-ending circle. The scraping and brushing of her rustic broom was softly rhythmic. A long cloak protected her from the biting wind. Kat felt transported into a moment happening centuries earlier.

She moved discreetly past the woman, who took no notice of either of them, and framed an image that captured the scene without showing the woman's face.

"Those brooms intrigue me, so I read up on them. I'm always amazed when I see street cleaners using them," Kat said. "They look ancient. They are just bundles of broom corn tied around a strong stick, and yet they still do such a good job."

They moved on, leaving the woman to her task. It was stumbling on moments like this, when the past came alive, that Kat loved so much about France.

"You were right. Being here is like stepping back in time. These squares are so small, not many people could ever have gathered outside. I keep imagining villagers rushing about their daily life with donkeys and carts and chickens in the streets. I can almost hear voices and see life happening, as if ghosts of the past are here."

Philippe nodded. "In villages like this, the intimacies of life could not be ignored," he said. "You lived your neighbors' lives: births, deaths and everything in between. Community was forced upon you, but no other way was known. Imagine the stories these walls could tell."

He pointed up at the citadel perched high above the town and suggested they leave the climb up to it for another day, when the weather was better.

"There is a zigzag walkway with twenty gates that goes along the town wall and up to the top. You can imagine what the view is like from up there. We'll hike it next time. And we'll come here on the Ducati."

Kat couldn't stop herself. "That would be perfect—as long as no one is after us."

Philippe began to apologize again but she interrupted. "Trust me, I'm working hard at getting over this, so forgive my pathetic attempts at humor."

He gave her a weak smile. "There's a motorcycle museum here but it's closed now for the winter. That's my pathetic attempt to distract you."

They shared a look that telegraphed their joint resolve to move on, for the moment, and turned into another deserted square.

Kat shivered and pulled the collar of her jacket around her neck. "It's so eerie and quiet here, except for the wind. I guess, for many, it's not a day to be out. A lot of these buildings look deserted, or at least sections of them do."

"Most of the people who live here year round are elderly, but in the summer you will find younger families as they visit parents and grandparents. Many of them own a building here, or at least a part of one, that's been passed down through the generations for centuries. Some of the houses are empty and have been for a long time because of the cost of modernizing and maintaining them."

Philippe tried his cellphone and snorted. "There never used to be good reception here but now everyone uses cellphones and the signal is pretty strong." He listened as Jacques gave him directions to his mother's house, then hung up.

"When I talked to him this morning, he told me it would be easier to tell us once we were in the village and now I see why."

They retraced their steps for a short distance, before turning into a narrow, flagstone street that took them between tall stucco houses joined side by side. Philippe stopped at a dark-green wooden door, the paint rich but weathered, with elaborate ancient brass keyholes, and climbed the four short, steep steps up to it. He rapped loudly. While they waited, he pointed to a low doorway leading off the street, and explained that it would have originally led to a donkey or goat stall and chicken roosts, below the living quarters.

Jacques opened the door and, after Philippe introduced him to Kat; he invited them in.

Tall, lean but strong-looking, and his face finely weathered, he might have been forty, Kat thought. His manner was easy and instantly familiar, more North American than French.

He ushered them into a sun-lit studio and introduced them to a statuesque, attractive, silver-haired woman of indeterminate age. "My mother, Véronique."

Kat later told Philippe that she had imagined an entirely different mother for Jacques. He confessed to the same.

"Enchantée." Véronique welcomed them, her green eyes softly probing, seeming to look into their souls. Her tone was gracious. "Philippe, I've heard about you for years. Jacques tells me you are the best fromager he knows." She spoke in French before turning and saying, in barely-accented English, "Katherine, I understand you are Canadian. Welcome. I hope you enjoyed the drive up here."

"More than you can possibly imagine," she said, and Philippe, standing just behind the others, rolled his eyes.

From the equipment in the room and the imaginative, artistic hangings on the stone walls, Kat deduced that Véronique was a talented weaver. Her eyes were captured by intriguing pieces of all sizes and colors, some earthy and others electric, crafted with unusual combinations of wools, silks, metallic threads, twigs and branches. A large wooden loom stood next to a window, beside wooden swifts and a spinning wheel. Véronique offered brief descriptions of their use.

His face lit with pride, Jacques told them his mother's work was much sought after, and she modestly smiled.

Kat began to relax in the hospitable atmosphere. She was curious and full of questions, which their hosts were happy to answer.

Véronique had studied fine arts in Paris as a young woman and had lived and worked in New York City for several years before returning to France with David, her American husband. They lived in Lyon for a few years before moving to the Côte d'Azur.

"Lyon is the cradle of weaving in Europe. I was fortunate to study under a true master for three years, and it was then that I discovered my own style. That was a very special time for me as an artist. The history is rich there, so be sure to visit it when you can. I'll be happy to give you some tips."

They chatted amiably for a while, then Véronique invited Kat and Philippe to stay for a late lunch of cassoulet. "David prepared it yesterday, before he left for Nice, after Jacques told me he would be stopping by today. It never makes sense to cook a small amount, so there is more than enough to go around. Please join us."

She led them through another large room, which she explained was her storage area, and they exclaimed at the bins and wicker baskets overflowing with brightly colored wools, silks, and other fibers. Wooden shelves bearing more yarn covered a long wall, the stacked skeins organized into a mosaic of vibrant and earthy hues. Kat felt her finger twitch; she was longing to take some shots.

They entered an enormous kitchen area with a vast working fireplace. Embers were glowing in its hearth, and it radiated warmth and a light, aromatic smell through the room. Pots hanging above the fire appeared to still be used for cooking, and a large collection of cookware and metal utensils hung from wall hooks, creating their own artistic statement.

"My husband loves cooking, thank goodness. When we lived in Lyon, and I was completely engrossed in my craft, he began taking cooking classes."

"Where better?" Philippe said.

Jacques broke into a broad smile. "You have to search long and hard to find a better meal than the ones mon père puts together. It's no wonder the three of us kids are all involved in work that is food-related."

Véronique added, "We have been the beneficiaries of his talent ever since."

In the center of the room was one of the longest wooden tables Kat had ever seen, surrounded by a collection of mostly unmatched wooden chairs. Jacques helped his mother set four places at one end.

"Do you mind if I take some photos in here after lunch?" Kat asked, her excitement overtaking her manners.

"Oh, please do," Véronique said. "We often forget how this room affects visitors. It has not changed much in three hundred years."

Jacques opened the tall shutters along one wall, exposing a huge window. "The only major change we made was to enlarge the windows," he said. "On nice days we can open the room up and look right down the valley. It's a magnificent view."

"Which got us into magnificent trouble," his mother added.

"And cost us a magnificent amount of money. You know the government does not allow changes to historic properties. It's a very long story, for another time."

"Let's talk about happier subjects," Véronique suggested, turning to ask Katherine how she had come to be living in France.

Philippe smiled shyly as Kat told the story of how they met first in the Luberon and their surprise at rediscovering each other in Antibes.

"It sounds like a love story to me," Jacques teased. Kat blushed.

Jacques served the sausage and white bean casserole piping hot from the cassole, a deep, conical earthenware pot, and set a baguette and a dish of simple greens on the table to accompany the meal. Kat leaned over her plate to inhale the rich aroma, which was almost as satisfying as eating the meal.

Over lunch, Véronique told them the history of the house. Like Philippe's property on the Cap d'Antibes, the building had been passed down in the family through the centuries. For long stretches it stood empty, but it was never abandoned. Twice a year, family members would set aside a few days to come here to repair and clean the house, generation after generation.

"Twenty years ago, when our children flew the nest, David and I decided to make this our weekend retreat and studio. He is a stressed-out businessman in Nice, when he is not cooking, and he enjoys getting away and hiking when he can. So this place suited both of our needs. I soon realized the light here was better for my work than in Nice, and the more time I spent here, the more inspired I was by my surroundings. For the last ten years we have lived here practically full-time. We just keep a pied-à-terre in la vieille ville in Nice."

Katherine glanced around the room again. "There's such character everywhere I look."

"It is a depository of departed souls and history, and we feel fortunate to live with all that," Véronique said.

Jacques added, "My wife hopes we will move here too one day, and create our own apartment upstairs. There is much more space than what you've seen. She doesn't want to stay in the high mountains forever, but for children growing up it's a better place than the city."

"And this is such an easy distance to commute to the coast."

Conversation flowed throughout the meal, much of it about gastronomie—tastes, smells, ingredients, plaisir.

Dessert was a slice of pumpkin cheesecake, served with a selection of chèvre and a bowl of fruit. Very "unFrancelike," as Kat commented later

"Cheesecake is a holdover from my years in America, and it's my husband's favorite dessert."

"Ma mère's home is seldom without one," Jacques said, a warm chuckle interrupting his words, "although it is mon père who makes it."

After coffee was poured, the two men became engrossed in a conversation about the cheese Jacques was crafting. Jacques was having some problems with new rules from the European Union and rhapsodized about his breed of goats, all individually named and apparently all handsome and intelligent.

Kat picked up her camera and wandered the kitchen and the studio next to it, taking photographs and admiring the wall hangings. Véronique answered Kat's many questions about her materials and techniques, as she walked with her. When they came back to the table, the men were still talking about cheese. Véronique and Katherine's eyes met and they smiled knowingly. "Qui se ressemble, s'assemble," Véronique whispered and then motioned to Katherine to sit at the table with her. "Birds of a feather ..." Kat whispered back, as she settled in a chair.

"Let me take you to the Cathedral while they solve the world problems, at least about cheese. It's just around the corner"—her eyes sparkled with mirth—"like everything else here."

"Philippe told me some of its history on the way up. I'd love to go."

"It will please you immensely. I noticed you are not just a point-and-shooter. You changed the setting often, and so quickly, when you were in the kitchen. May I see some of those shots?"

Kat passed the camera to her, showing her where to touch the screen to move the photos along.

"You are a serious artist, Katherine. That's easy to see," Véronique said.

Philippe looked up for a moment and nodded vigorously. "Sans aucun doute!"

"He misses nothing," Véronique observed. "I like that."

"So do I," Kat replied, feeling blessed to be here, with him.

Véronique put her hand on Philippe's shoulder. "I am taking your amoureuse to Notre-Dame de l'Assomption. Carry on with your shop talk."

"It has a simple Gothic exterior, just four hundred years old," Véronique said as they approached the cathedral, which was no bigger than a church. Two small olive trees flanked its entrance, and the women walked between them up to a massive, dark wood double door. Katherine drew in a deep breath and closed her eyes briefly. "They remind me of the doors to La Chapelle Saint-Bernardin in Antibes."

The doors were elaborately carved with details from the town's military past. Katherine couldn't resist rubbing her palm lightly over a helmet, sword and stirrups featured on one panel. Véronique smiled. "I do the same. It's almost irresistible, n'est-ce pas? One feels an instant connection to the craftsmen of centuries past who created these works of art."

"I feel almost transported to the time the work was done," Kat said. "They lived the history and emotion they've expressed in their work. It's very powerful."

They went inside and Kat was stunned. Belied by its simple exterior, this holy place was filled with exquisite, intricate, religious artwork. Above the altar hung a huge painting of the assumption that was clearly centuries old, but Kat's attention was caught by the domed ceiling above it, which was painted a luminescent provençal blue, supported by gilded ribs, and dotted with stars. "It's hypnotic," she said. "Like I'm walking into a dream."

The cathedral's subtle lighting accentuated the detailed stained glass windows and the copious gold trim, but somehow the rich excess of the decoration still seemed humble.

"I can't get over finding such a treasure, tucked away in a village like this, with absolutely no tourists here. It feels surreal to be standing here, and a great honor."

"I feel the same way, Katherine. I come here for inspiration some days, for peace and meditation others. I seldom leave without noticing some detail that cries out for me to interpret it. It can be something as basic as a shade of color, a ray of light, or as ornate as a carving or sculpture. This place is a treasure chest of ingenuity, not just spirituality."

"Have you read *The Pillars of the Earth*?" Katherine asked, reminded of Ken Follett's novel about the building of an English cathedral in the Middle Ages.

"Mon Dieu, I loved that novel," Véronique said.

On their way back, they met Philippe and Jacques. "We made the cheese transfer in the parking lot so we can leave anytime," Philippe said. "Is that fine with you, Kat?"

"I hate to go but we've already stayed much longer than we expected. I hope we didn't spoil your plans for the day. I've had such a wonderful time."

"My truck broke down for a very good reason," Jacques laughed

Véronique held Katherine's hand, squeezing it gently.

"Please come back any time and stay longer, now you know where we are. The more time you spend here, the more stories your eye will discover. We are not surrounded by the same type of intoxicating beauty you find on the coast, or the charm and sensuous landscape of

Provence. There's much beauty here that only shows itself if you take the time to become familiar with the village and its past."

"There's a completely different enchantment here. A captivating allure."

Véronique's face lit up with enthusiasm. "I have an idea! Some friends—artists who live in the area—are coming here on Friday. I know it's only three days from now, short notice, but we take turns at each other's places once a month to share ideas. We begin with coffee early in the morning and go out for a walk with our sketchpads and cameras. We come back for lunch and eat and talk and talk and eat. Why don't you come the night before so you can join us? It would be my pleasure to have you stay here."

Kat was surprised by the invitation so soon after meeting Véronique, but she had felt a kinship from the beginning. Perhaps the artistic sensibility they shared, and the North American influence when it comes to hospitality, was behind the offer.

She looked briefly at Philippe. He seemed pleased.

"Merci mille fois, Véronique! How kind of you. I will come for sure."

Jacques insisted on walking back to the car with them, where he thanked Philippe again for coming out of his way to meet him. He stood waving as they drove off.

"Being back in the car and driving normally feels very weird," Kat said.

"Very," Philippe agreed.

"Except for your reaction to that note and those minutes of terror on the way here, I would say this has been a perfect day."

"Saying I'm sorry doesn't feel like it's enough now, and it isn't."

"Okay, let's move on," Kat said, unsure whether fear or strength was powering her words. "You asked me to wait and I will, but give me a time frame. A day? A week? Two weeks?"

"Please. Don't bind me to a specific date. It's been on my mind all afternoon. I have to make some phone calls but I have a plan—of sorts."

"This is driving me crazy so I'm simply going to try to stop speculating. I'll keep waiting until you are ready to tell me everything—

or until I can't any longer. I'm not asking about it now. Period. Now let's talk about Jacques and his mother. What an intriguing woman she is." Kat found that easy to say and was surprised she did. She couldn't believe she was being so calm about it. The old her wouldn't have reacted like this.

There was much to recap from the afternoon, although Philippe kept drifting off into moments of silent preoccupation.

"Véronique is such a warm and engaging woman—as modest as she is talented. I liked her a lot and I'm thrilled at her invitation to come back on Friday."

"Bien sûr! It's a wonderful opportunity. The more I watch you with your camera, the more I realize what an artist you are."

"I've always thought of it as a hobby, but I've taken lots of courses and read a ton about it. It really is an important part of me. My eyes are always taking pictures even when I don't have a camera with me."

"It didn't take Véronique long to recognize that quality in you."

"She made it easy to feel comfortable with her. Jacques too. Their hospitality felt more North American. I mean, I find the French warm, in their own way—you know I do—but it usually takes them longer to open up. I guess her years in the States and marrying an American have something to do with it."

Philippe nodded. "Oui, d'accord. I've known Jacques for years. He has a farm farther up in the mountains where he keeps his goats, makes his special cheese, and lives very simply with his wife and children. He's always quiet-spoken but today he was forthcoming. He told me that his father had lost a tremendous amount of money in the financial disaster of a few years ago, so even though he is over eighty, he still runs his business in Nice. Finances were a major reason his parents moved to Entrevaux. I was surprised he told me this about his family."

Kat smiled. "Today was a good reminder about not making assumptions. I had pictured Jacques as a short, stocky mountain-type who would be quite terse. I was sure his mother would be frail and in need of assistance. Don't ask me why, but I did."

"You just never know," Philippe said. "She's another beautiful and engaging woman whose age does not define her, and I mean that in the most complimentary way." He reached over and pulled Kat close to him.

She reached up and kissed his cheek, gently moving his hand from her breast. "I know you do. I hear you and I love you, but keep your eyes on the road and your hands on the steering wheel, please. And promise to stop at all railroad crossings."

Philippe stared at her, surprised she could joke about it.

Kat stared back, surprised at herself.

Still holding her hand near her breast, Philippe said, "Only if you promise we will continue from this point when we are home."

Kat rolled her eyes. "That's one way to take our minds off whatever is going on." She traced her finger up his thigh, lightly grazing the rise in his jeans. "I'll be happy to keep that promise."

The radio was tuned to TSF Jazz, dusk was settling in and the drive was a quiet one—a good quiet. There was not a further word about the drive up. Kat's hand rested lightly on Philippe's neck, her fingers gently massaging from time to time.

Back in Antibes, they made a quick stop at Philippe's storage unit to drop off the crate of cheese, but as they pulled into their parking space at home, Kat felt him tense up. She said nothing, nor did he. Once in the apartment, they agreed they were not hungry.

"How about crêpes in an hour or so, Chouchou? I have some ratatouille we could eat with them."

"Bonne idée."

Kat settled in the window seat in the salon, her favorite reading spot, while Philippe sat down at his computer. Not long afterward he left the room, carrying his phone.

Kat promised herself not to say another word about the note until he was ready to talk. Not to Philippe anyway. Molly was another story, and she was going to Skype her tomorrow.

Three hours later, they were both tidying the kitchen before bed.

Philippe gathered her into his arms and kissed her lightly before brushing his cheek on her hair. "Here I go, apologizing again," he said. "I'm sorry for everything that happened today. I can't say it enough. I was shocked by that note and didn't handle the situation well and the unbelievable problem on the road—what can I say? The worst part is that I put you at such danger."

Kat was about to speak when her eyes welled with tears. A lump in her throat stopped the words. Philippe pulled his head back. He could see she was on the verge of crying. Kat looked away.

"Non, Minou, non," he murmured. "Go ahead, cry. You have every right to."

Kat found her voice by looking down. "Our conversation this morning took me back to a very bad place in my marriage, and that's bothering me more than anything." She sniffed, unable to hold back her tears or disguise the sadness in her voice.

Philippe wiped away the tears and lifted her chin. "I want to wake up beside you every morning for the rest of my life," he said. "Always remember that. This problem will go away."

She wanted to believe him. "Entrevaux this afternoon was so special. Let's just think about that and forget the rest for now. I mean it. I'm so glad you took me there."

In the bedroom, he turned back the covers and held out his hand.

Kat closed her eyes, savoring his scent, as they folded into each other.

They made love slowly and sweetly before drifting off to sleep.

4

Nothing terribly out of the ordinary had occurred in the two days since the frightening episode on the way to Entrevaux. The only thing different Kat was aware of was that Philippe was spending much more time privately on the phone.

Both days she had arrived at the market to discover Gilles taking care of business and Philippe in the storage unit on his cell. His not serving his customers personally indicated to her the gravity of the matter, but she was sticking to her vow and was being tight-lipped. She had to trust what he had promised her. She could see that he was doing his best to keep their lives together calm and happy. Whatever he was doing to take care of the problem, he was doing away from home. She could only hope it was working.

That summer, Kat had become accustomed to eating outdoors on warm summer evenings and now the addition of heaters on terraces still made it possible. The socializing was as important as the dining. The sense of community that she felt in this ancient town grew as waiters and other locals greeted her, not just at meals but also during the day, after just over a week.

The few times they had eaten dinner at home, both of them prepped and laughed as they enjoyed the intimacy of it all. One evening the ingredients were left on the counter as their appetite for desire caused a delay in the dinner hour.

Philippe was a master of the grill. The day's catch was his favorite plat du jour. No matter where they dined, he'd teach Kat about various aspects of French culture, such as the philosophy of terroir.

"It's a term most often used about our wines," he said as they sipped a crisp white from Cassis, "but really it encompasses everything about our obsession with food. It is simply a history or tradition, a combination of local factors, like soil, climate, and altitude, that makes what we eat and drink unique."

"Like these amazing wines from Cassis?"

"D'accord." Philippe raised his glass in a salute. "It's something about a product that enhances community, cooking and taste. C'est tout. Like the chickens from Bourg-en-Bresse or butter from Normandy, melons from Cavaillon."

"Or all of those delicious cheeses you've introduced me too that are made from the milk of a cow that is only fed certain grasses and herbs by nubile young maidens singing soft lullabies at dusk," she teased.

"You get the picture," he laughed.

Katherine got the picture every day at the market once she understood the importance of *terroir*. The average shopper's knowledge of local foods was comprehensive, and their decisions about what to buy were often based upon origins.

"I've got my work cut out for me," she told Philippe as they sat down to lunch one day. "I thought I was a pretty good cook but I rarely paid much attention to where the food I bought came from. With a fussy husband who only wanted basic meat-and-potato meals, I had no reason to be adventurous about what I ate. Olives, for example, those black ones and red and brown –"

"This can't be true," he said, looking startled, as he set a small bowl on the table. "You've never eaten any other olive than a little green one?"

She shook her head. "Don't ask me why, but whenever they were offered, I simply passed them by."

"But you served them at your buffet dinatoire in Sainte Mathilde, non?"

Katherine smiled as she recalled that little cocktail party she hosted her last night in the farmhouse outside Sainte Mathilde, on her first exchange. She had invited Joy and her family and Philippe and a few others who had been so kind and welcoming to her for those two weeks.

Now her face reddened with embarrassment. She paused before admitting, "When Joy first took me to the market, she was so enthusiastic about the choice of olives and the tapenade, that I put some in my basket but never ate them. I didn't want to admit my ignorance about them. To be honest, I didn't know what tapenade was apart from the fact it was made with olives."

"Ahhh, but you haven't tasted olives like the ones we have here," he said with a teasing smile as he popped one in his mouth. "Straight from the tree is definitely not recommended, but once olives are cured and seasoned, they are precious bursts of flavor. Try this one."

One proved not to be enough, and in a matter of days Kat found she had a new addiction. She had begun to work her way through the many choices at the market. Like so many other foods in France, the simple, artistic ways olives were displayed invited her to try them.

Philippe's friend, Emile, was a popular olive vendor at the market. He arranged glistening mounds of black, green, red and brown olives, some herby, some spicy, others fruity, in large, colorful ceramic bowls. Long-handled olive wood scoops rested on top, creating a visual Kat had photographed many times. The tastes were equally inviting. His varieties of tapenade were legendary, and he closely guarded their recipes.

"Goutez! Trust me and taste," Emile would cajole his customers. It was a rare person who bought without trying first, and he was a master at coaxing customers to his counter.

Philippe would bring home just the right cheese to go with the type of olives Kat had bought. She was hooked on these small fruits that were such a staple here. After sampling them all, she especially loved tapenade, and in particular the traditional Provençal combination of finely crushed black olives, capers, anchovies, garlic and olive oil with a touch of lemon and thyme, spread on a fresh baguette.

They would talk for hours together. For Kat, it was a refreshing change from the long periods of silence she had endured during her marriage.

There were times Kat found it hard not to dwell on what might be behind the mysterious note and the frightening chase on the way to Entrevaux. She even tried to convince herself the chase might have been the result of mistaken identity. Maybe Philippe was paranoid because of the note and had overreacted—big-time. To distract herself from these thoughts, she would get her camera and turn her mind to observing people and places in and around Antibes.

The more accustomed she became to her surroundings, the more her eyes were drawn to the little details: the texture and color of the ancient cobblestones; the grain of a wooden door; an intricate metal keyhole; the angles of loose shutters; the variety of shades of terracotta in the clay roof tiles; the peeling paint and the marks of centuries of wear. She found beauty and artistry in the little things all around her.

Now autumn had settled in, the lower angle of the light and the withering of vegetation offered her new perspectives, and she returned to her favorite places to photograph the transformations.

One evening, while they were both working at their computers, Kat remarked, "I still cannot get over how much I use my camera almost every day now. It's become part of my life here. It's because I have much more time for it now, but it's also because my eye is drawn to everything around me here. Even the fruits and vegetables look more appealing."

Philippe drew his chair next to hers. "You know, you've only shown me a few shots here and there. It's time I had a complete retrospective."

Kat pulled up the file in which she kept what she considered her best work from her growing collection, and the slideshow was on.

Philippe watched it intently and with growing enthusiasm.

"You must take these to André at his gallery and let him see your work," he said. "I'm serious."

Kat thanked him, but she thought his opinion was sweetly biased.

"I'm just a picture-taker," she said.

5

Late in the afternoon on Thursday, two days after their trip to Entrevaux, Katherine kissed Philippe goodbye. She was going back to visit Véronique overnight.

"This is the first night we'll be apart," he said. "I'll miss you!"

"And I you, Chouchou! I'm excited though. Thanks for encouraging me to go. I imagine I will have a much calmer trip this time but I will watch out for black SUVs!"

Philippe looked chagrined.

She packed several wines and cheeses, carefully chosen by Philippe, and set off, using the GPS to point the way through Antibes to route E80.

She cranked up the volume for an album of her favorite songs by French jazz singer Zaz and sang along, filling the car with happy energy. One of the things she loved about driving alone was being able to sing at the top of her lungs.

The song felt like her anthem now—love, joy, good spirits. That's the happiness she had in her life now, or so she thought. She wished she knew what was going on and why he would say that she might not want to stay. Those were the words she wanted to forget.

The first rays of sunset were brushing the high, jagged peaks ahead with pink after she left the E80 for the road up to Entrevaux. She felt carefree as she left the traffic and the road carried her up into the wild, remote hills. Hairpin curves demanded her focus.

But despite her efforts not to dwell on the previous trip up this road, her thoughts kept flickering back to them. First to Philippe's discovery of the note on the car and then to what now seemed like a bad dream: the terrifying moments in the car.

"A frickin' car chase? And no cops involved after?" had been Molly's incredulous reaction when they Skyped the day after the trip to Entrevaux. Kat had shared every detail, and they had tried to come up with some logical explanation, to no avail. Molly agreed with Kat that she should be patient and wait for Philippe's explanation. "As long as you are safe, girlfriend." Kat had assured Molly that she was. She didn't mention his saying she might not want to stay with him. She couldn't say that out loud. Not even to Molly.

Blowing out a long sigh now, Kat brought her attention once again to the sharp turns on the road and felt a shiver run up her spine as she drove through the railroad crossing.

Soon the road straightened and she was in the deep valley overlooked by the fort at Entrevaux.

She left the car at the parking lot at the train station and walked up the hill to the gatehouse. Unable to resist, she set down the cooler and the overnight bag she was carrying to take a few photos in the dying light.

Once across the bridge, she felt the same thrill walking under the ancient portcullis as before. She walked up to the first square, certain she would find the green door to Véronique's house without a problem.

Minutes later, back in the main square, she made a phone call. "I'm going in circles. Au secours! Help!"

Véronique directed her to wait on the bench by the fountain and, within no time, tapped her on the shoulder.

"I was that close?"

"You and everyone else the first time they come back."

They dropped Katherine's bag at the house and decided to go for a walk through the town in the dying light. Along the way, Véronique charmed and fascinated her with stories of some of the families who had lived here for generations.

They ate dinner at the cozy bistro she and Philippe had noted on their visit. The wine flowed freely, and when the owner brought a tray loaded with piquant cheeses to the table, Véronique invited him and his wife, friends of hers, to join them. Since they were the only customers, another bottle of wine appeared.

"Un cadeau—a gift," the proprietor said with a smile.

The conversation rolled on, drifting between French and English and shifting seamlessly from one topic to another.

Katherine asked about their life in Entrevaux. She was reminded once more how much this country's history was engrained in the lives of its citizens with so many families keeping roots in an area for hundreds of years.

As the two women strolled back to the house, their conversation turned to art and to what inspired them most for their own work. Once they were seated at the kitchen table, over a nightcap of Cognac, Véronique started to talk intimately about how growing old made her feel and how, as her sex life diminished, her artistry grew.

Kat was embarrassed at first, even though she realized it was a normal topic for Véronique and not meant to make her uncomfortable.

"We French have a very open attitude to our bodies and sex and how we relate to them," Véronique said. "I'm sorry, I did not mean to make you uneasy."

Katherine waved her hand. "No, no. Please continue. I know the French talk about these issues much more matter of factly, but sometimes I still react like a Canadian."

"I am seventy-five, much older than you. I know that life changes at this stage, and, yet, I'm always a little surprised when it happens to me. I feel much younger, but the realities are what they are. David is five years older. Physically he struggles a little more each year, and losing his sexual prowess has been difficult for him."

Katherine shifted her position, hoping the move and her discomfort went unnoticed.

"But here is what is satisfying now," Véronique continued. "We have both adjusted. What has become much more intense to us—our passion, you might say—is the beauty of life around us and the importance of what we share. Do you suppose it's because we are acutely aware of time slipping by?"

Without waiting for an answer, she went on. "Our lives have a different intensity now. Our lust is for life, for beauty and peace and, of course … le plaisir. I am often told I have never created better work than in these past few years. David spends less time running his business but gets more pleasure from his successes and is less disappointed when things don't work out. I think we have never loved each other more …"

Her voice trailed off.

"May we all age so well and so wisely," Kat said.

"Pardon my ramblings," Véronique hiccupped behind her hand, "but I'm caught off guard by the revelations of old age. The Cognac urged me to share it with you. Now, I will show you to the guest room, and please let me know if there is anything you need."

"It's been a lovely evening and an illuminating conversation. You expressed so beautifully how life can continue to be satisfying and even exciting, just in different ways. Thank you."

"Make no mistake, ma chère, there are many who continue to enjoy sex at my age too. Everyone is different."

Katherine smiled, "Taking it one day at a time is the secret."

"D'accord," Véronique agreed, leaning in to bise her.

In the guest room, the window was open wide, and cool mountain air washed over Katherine as she slipped under a heavy duvet. Instead of the sea air she loved, this was another kind of good, she thought: a fresh, crisp breeze, cooled by the snow-tipped mountain summits. The quiet was a dramatic change from the sounds of the sea, traffic and people that were her lullabies in Antibes.

In the stillness, she heard the distant bark of a dog and she smiled as she drifted off. It never fails, there are always dogs, was her last thought.

Morning came quickly and a light rap on her door roused her from delicious sleep.

After a quick shower, she went to the kitchen, where she found Véronique had lit a fire. The aroma of bacon being cooked filled the room.

"It's the easiest meal—breakfast in a pan—again from David's childhood and transported across the Atlantic. Lardons ... our bacon, eggs, peppers, onions, cheese, all cooked in a skillet. I'll keep it warm in the oven and plate it when the others are here. It's hearty fare, but they won't allow me to prepare anything else. They've heard what a terrible cook I am, so this is my spécialité de la maison!"

"It smells divine."

"My secret ingredient is Jacques' young goat cheese. It has a unique flavor. The others will be here soon and I'm looking forward to you meeting them."

The day proved to be as invigorating as Véronique had promised. The group was friendly, focused, just a bit eccentric, and very French.

It was not merely a social gathering but a serious sharing of creative ideas about inspiration and technique. There were good-natured exchanges and a lot of laughter as they hiked the chosen path for the morning. They stopped several times along the way, either just to look around or to draw, photograph, or simply make notes.

Lunch, which they took turns carrying in a few baskets, consisted of baguette and a selection of cheeses, bowls of tapenade and olives, assorted sliced hams, and the customary salad of greens dressed with vinaigrette.

The others were curious about the visitor in their midst and some of the questions they asked Kat pushed her to think about the why and how of her photography. She tried to explain her approach, helped by translation at times. She enjoyed being treated as an artist in her own right and hoped she sounded like she knew what she was doing.

The group was made up of two painters, a sculptor, a potter, another weaver and a photographer who shot only in black and white.

With one exception, everyone had brought a computer or a tablet with them, so it was easy to share photos of their work in progress with each other. The exception was the potter, Norman Joliette, who worked strictly from pencil sketches, photos and notes. Véronique explained he had an assistant who took care of any computer-related work.

The others in the group introduced him, with obvious affection, as l'ermite, because, they said, he preferred to use his bicycle for transportation and still had a dial telephone.

After they returned to the house later that afternoon, Norman sought Kat out.

"I'm not a hermit," he told her as Véronique translated. "I simply decided to remove myself from social media and cellphones, and I like to bike wherever I go."

Another added, to laughter from the others, including Norman, "If my vehicle was a thirty-year-old Volkswagen hippie mobile, I might prefer to cycle too."

Norman spoke happily of the quiet refuge in the hills where he created his work and where agents came by regularly to place orders for shops and private clients. He had walked away from a shop on a busy street in Cannes when he grew tired of crowds and traffic. Now he rented a stall at a different craft fair every two months to sell his wares and build his customer list.

It struck Kat as a perfect example of choosing to make a change, although Norman's change had been rather extreme and had caused his wife to leave him. He told her not to fear change. If he could change his life this dramatically, so could she.

"Crois en toi-même et en ton art," he said.

Véronique translated: "Believe in yourself and your art."

Norman was much quieter than the others but just as encouraging when they looked at Kat's work. They all agreed she should exhibit her work and focus on it full time.

"Your talent is obvious. If you are in a position to make photography your life, then why not?" one of them said, speaking for all of them.

"I have much to learn," she demurred.

"Where better than the south of France?" they all said, in one way or another. "Who could ask for more exquisite light?"

Driving home late that afternoon, Kat was overflowing with ideas. She asked herself the same questions. Should she pursue photography seriously? Why not? If everything else in her life was changing, why not this too? Just because her paid work had always been science-related, who said she couldn't change that?

6

Katherine's birthday was on November 11th. Philippe was playful about how to commemorate the day.

"I always thought the band and parade on Armistice Day were to honor those who gave everything for our country but this year they will be honoring you too," he joked.

It made Kat think about all the birthdays during her marriage that her husband had barely acknowledged. Her parents always made an occasion of the date, but, even though she always had a birthday gift for him, James only ever gave her a card. When he remembered. So she reveled in the attention Philippe was showering upon her.

She awoke on her birthday to the sight of a vase of sunflowers on her bedside table. She lay in bed for a few minutes with the shutters flung open to welcome the morning sun, and considered how fine her fifty-seven years felt.

After she got up, she found that Philippe had left a pain aux raisins for her when he slipped back with the flowers. It was still warm and she ate it as she planned what she would do for the morning. She was keeping her promise not to ask Philippe about his problem and had begun to relax about it.

The weather had turned surprisingly mild that day, and a sweatshirt tied over her shoulders was all she needed as she walked to the market after yoga.

"Joyeux anniversaire, mon amour. Happy birthday, Minou!"

Wrapping her tightly in his arms, he announced to his customers that it was her birthday. They applauded and offered her their best wishes.

He lowered his voice and turned away from the lineup awaiting his attention. "I invite you for a special birthday déjeuner when I am home from here. À vélo. D'accord?" She grinned at the idea of a bicycle lunch.

Back at the apartment, after an invigorating shower, she laid her cycling clothes on the bed and, as a treat to herself, spent the rest of the morning on the window seat in the salon, wrapped in her robe and with her head buried in a book. Here, heavy wooden shutters opened to the busy boulevard below. Traffic was much quieter now that the majority of tourists were gone, but she could still hear the clatter of dishes and cutlery and the scraping of furniture as waiters at nearby restaurants set up for the lunch crowd.

At one point, she raised her head from her book to listen to the lively chatter and laughter of students leaving the école secondaire around the corner. Later she moved to the small table for two in an alcove off the kitchen and opened the shutters to look down the cobbled passageway that dog-legged between ancient buildings, all jumbled into one. Neighbors were leaning over their windowsills to chat with another across the narrow lane, and the sounds of conversation and of someone playing the piano floated through the air. Philippe was oblivious to the beauty of this simple scene, Kat knew, as he had lived with it all his life, but she loved to witness it every day. He had chuckled at her explanation.

"It's so completely different from what I'm used to. It's so European. I love it."

Molly had laughed too when they talked about it, and Kat told her she didn't really listen to what people were saying to each other. "That's your fu– well, your classic Canadian personality shining through," Molly said. "You're too polite to eavesdrop."

"Of course, sometimes I can't help hearing, but I'm not trying to listen in. Honest!"

Eavesdropping made her feel uncomfortable. The voices and words were an ongoing background, an audible tapestry of lives being lived.

Philippe teased her. "Mais non! Gossip was how news was spread for centuries. Everyone listened to everyone else's business. Everyone still does!"

Now she heard a cat meowing, and she peered into the alley, leaning over the planter of sage, basil and thyme she was growing and breathed in the aromas.

There were often distant as well as nearby yowls and cries from cats, she noted, but seldom constant yapping from dogs. The village dogs seemed far better behaved than those of some of her neighbors in Toronto. She decided it was probably because village dogs were allowed to wander. They were happy.

"Bien sûr!" her new friend, Annette, had agreed when they were hiking one day. She had met Annette through the cycling club and then discovered they went to the same yoga studio. Their friendship was slowly becoming more personal. This was, she knew, often the French way: a quiet approach until they felt ready to invite you closer.

Annette was a researcher with an environmental science company in nearby Sophia-Antipolis, and they shared a common history of education with science degrees. Much of the week she worked from home and could pick and choose her hours.

Annette had laughed and nodded when Katherine said she had noticed that picking up dog poop seemed to be a problem, especially for the person walking the dog.

"That's why walking in France requires picking your path carefully. Les crottes de chiens! Le caca! Those cute chiens like to poop as they make their rounds. Picking up after them is starting to happen slowly over here, but we do have signs now and even the odd poop station."

Kat let the sounds from outside envelop her again, and her thoughts turned to her mother, who had always been the first person to call her on her birthday. She missed her.

She took a clementine from a bowl, and as she peeled it and its scent became stronger so did warm memories of times with anyu, the

Hungarian word for mother she always used. She recalled her mother telling her on her last birthday how much it meant to receive a simple orange as a gift in the months right after the war, in 1945. This conversation occurred soon after James had left her, while they were lingering over one of her mother's appetizing Hungarian dishes in the warm, comfy kitchen.

"My darling Katica, we live life thinking we will always be able to do everything we want but before we know it, old age catches up with us. We find ourselves grasping the outer edge of the time we have left. Don't let this injury James has inflicted stop you from living life, from seeing what else is out there for you," Elisabeth had said, a knowing look in her eyes as she reached to take her daughter's hand. "I trust there is more. There is always more."

At the time Katherine had not believed there was anything else out there for her. But her mother had been right.

The tantalizing aroma of paprika that often filled her mother's kitchen now suddenly seemed to fill her nostrils, and she decided to make chicken paprikash for Philippe. Winter was coming. The time was right.

With her thoughts grounded in the past for the moment, Kat made another decision that surprised her more than anything: The next time she was in Toronto, she would speak with James. Face to face.

She watched a couple walking their bikes down the lane below the window and thought about how much she enjoyed cycling. The rhythm of her body's movements, her breath, and the sense of being in a world of her own always freed her from the constraints that often inhibited her reflections. She had been putting a lot of thought into how things had ended with James and why she had avoided any contact with him since then.

There was her mother's voice again. What doesn't kill us makes us stronger.

Kat knew she was stronger. She knew she was now capable of meeting James, and she had some words to say to this man who had taken so much of her life and discarded it so hurtfully.

Her time in France and Philippe's love were allowing her to see for the first time the woman she really was.

She definitely had a few words for James.

Philippe rushed home in the early afternoon and they were soon on their bikes. The day called for warm clothes, but the sky was its classic blue and the sun shone brightly.

When they reached a favorite spot by the sea, they followed the narrow, well-worn path to a grassy patch near large flat rocks. Resting their bikes against a tree, they reminisced about being there in October, when Kat had planned to leave for Toronto.

"It seems like a lifetime ago," she told him, her eyes glistening. "You have changed my world, and I thank you for that."

After Kat spread the picnic blanket, Philippe opened a bottle of champagne and they toasted her birthday, their love, and the delicious food he had prepared, still hidden in the picnic basket.

"I get lost in your eyes. You make me so happy, so full of life again. This is just the first of many, many celebrations we will share," he said.

For a while they sat basking in the sun and in the loveliness surrounding them. The view across the bay to where the medieval stone towers of Antibes were outlined against the layers of hills behind was one of Kat's favorites. They chatted, carefree and relaxed, about nothing in particular until Philippe got up and unstrapped the picnic basket from his bike.

"Ferme les yeux!" he ordered, and she covered her eyes. "Voilà!"

He laid out on olive wood platters a baguette and her favorite foie gras, as well as sardines in oil and lemon, sliced melon with prosciutto, figs and a small pot of crème brûlée. Her eyes went directly to a heart-shaped cheese in the midst of the feast.

"Did you cut it like that, just for me, for us?"

"Mais non! But I chose it just for us. This is Neufchatel from the Haute Normandie region; its lineage goes back to 1035. You're going to love the history of this. During the Hundred Years War –"

"The fourteenth and fifteenth centuries!" Kat interrupted with a grin, pleased she remembered the dates.

"Oui, ma petite history buff. The French farm girls fell in love with English soldiers sent to Normandy and they made the cheese heart-shaped for them. It was one way they could communicate their feelings. The recipe was protected by the Appellation d'Origine Contrôlée just a few years ago, and now it can only be made using warm milk from a Normandy breed of cow."

She leaned toward him and planted a lingering kiss. "You give your cheeses such a life with these stories. I love it."

"Et moi, I love that you love it. I never knew my cheese could be so séduisant." He narrowed his eyes and uttered the last word with a cheeky grin.

She gave him a look that showed just how seductive she found him and his cheese stories.

He asked her to put the Neufchatel on a small plate he was holding. As she did, she saw a small parchment envelope that had been hidden beneath it. It was the kind he often used to package slices of cheese.

"Do you need this?" she asked.

"Non … c'est pour toi, Minou," he said, with a shy smile.

Kat reached in and removed a delicate gold charm bracelet along with a folded note. Philippe had written, "En amour, un et un font un. There may be more beautiful times, but this one is ours. (JP Sartre)"

Her eyes brimmed with tears, " Such tender words."

Philippe pulled her into his embrace. He was aware of a hesitation from Kat from time to time, and he sensed she was still protecting her heart, whether she realized it or not.

He kissed away the few tears that slipped down her cheeks, before their lips came together for a long, slow kiss.

When they finally put some space between them, Philippe slipped the bracelet from Katherine's hand. "Regarde. I even managed to find cheese for you here."

Kat laughed as he showed her a golden wedge-shaped charm. "What do you think? A Brie, perhaps? And this Eiffel Tower is for, well, France. And this heart is because you have mine forever."

Feeling like her own heart would burst, she held out her wrist for him to clasp the bracelet around. Then she carefully zipped his note into a pocket on her shirt.

"Merci, mon amour. Je l'adore ... et je t'adore."

They did not linger over lunch and were soon cycling home with one thing on their minds. The language of their desire required no translation.

7

The next morning, the ring of Philippe's cell phone jolted them both out of deep sleep at 5:17 a.m.

Philippe listened for a moment then spoke briefly into the phone, his voice filled with alarm. He leapt out of bed.

"What's wrong?" she asked as he began pulling on his clothes.

"That was Gilles. Our storage unit is on fire."

"Is he okay?"

"Oui, grâce à Dieu! He went early to meet a delivery and when he opened the door, a small explosion knocked him off his feet and started a fire."

"I'll go with you."

"Let me dash now, and I'll call to let you know what's going on. Gilles said everything is under control. The firefighters are there, and Mercier is waiting to talk to us. Looks like we'll lose quite a bit of product."

Mercier was the local chief of police and was always called by just his last name. Philippe had described him as someone everyone trod lightly around but whose word was his bond. At least, Philippe hoped it was.

"This is crazy," he said as he headed out the door.

The market was buzzing with speculation when Kat joined Philippe and Gilles later.

Coffee, baguette sandwiches and pastries had been arriving at their stand all morning as they were visited by everyone they knew, and seemingly by every employee at the local constabulary, fire department and the mayor's office.

"An event like this involves the entire community," Philippe explained. "Everyone takes it personally –"

"And has their own theory," Gilles interrupted.

Gilles appeared quite relaxed about the incident, now that the shock had passed. "I think it was a short in the wiring of the new security system for the whole bank of storage units. It was just my misfortune to get knocked over by it."

Philippe did not look convinced. "That's what the police and firefighters are saying, but some expert is coming tomorrow from Nice to investigate."

"The insurance will cover the losses," Gilles added. "Except nothing can cover the fine Mont d'Or that was delivered last week. We will have to wait another year for a perfectly aged supply of that."

The two men seemed more crestfallen at this prospect than at anything else. Had the rest of the incident not been so serious, Kat would have smiled.

They spent the remainder of the day sorting out the salvageable cheeses. Emile, the olive vendor, had an extra unit with refrigeration that was almost empty and immediately insisted they use it. With all the help they were offered, they got most things in order by late afternoon. Philippe even found time to fill out a mountain of insurance forms, a pile of paper that was typical of the French bureaucracy. After the market closed, everyone gathered at the local family-run Italian restaurant, which the owners closed to the public for a long and loud meal, where the wine flowed freely.

Philippe spent the next day meeting with more investigators and insurance representatives, and he, Kat, and Gilles continued the clean-up. As news of the incident spread to his suppliers, many of them went out of their way to bring more product to him and stay for a supportive drink from an endless supply of rosé. The incident was the headline news in the local paper.

Philippe and Kat had planned a weekend in Sainte Mathilde to visit their friend, Joy Lallibert and her family. Joy, originally from England, had helped Kat so much during her first home exchange earlier that year and had been responsible for her introduction to Philippe. The weekend would continue Kat's birthday celebration. After much debate, they decided to stick to their plan and go, in spite of everything.

"There's nothing more to be done anyway. Gilles' father is a builder, and the two of them will begin to fix the damage this morning. With what we moved into Emile's storage space and the new deliveries that arrived yesterday, Gilles will be able to keep the stall open all weekend."

"Business as usual?" Kat asked.

"With a slightly reduced inventory."

Joy had called Philippe's cell yesterday after she heard about the explosion to make sure the two of them were all right.

"News travels fast in these parts," Joy explained. "We are all very upset and hope that electrical problem will be fixed. It's a good thing the entire bank of storage units did not go up in smoke. I tried Philippe's phone several times but it just went to voicemail."

Katherine gave her a detailed description of everything that was happening and assured her they were still coming for a visit.

"Merveilleux! It will be good for you both to get away from that commotion."

Now Kat said to Philippe, "The change of scene will do us both good, and I'm so looking forward to seeing everyone, including Pico, of course."

"I think the Lallibert's dog fell in love with you just like I did," Philippe quipped.

A smile lit up Kat's face. "Who knew that a soppy yellow Lab would find his way into my heart so completely?"

Kat's excitement mounted as soon as she recognized the countryside near Sainte Mathilde. The drive of just over two hours always pleased her. After leaving the coast and the rugged red rocks of le massif de l'Esterel, the countryside changed dramatically. Vineyards, orchards, olive groves and fields stretched toward a backdrop of rolling hills. Perched villages came and went from view as the road twisted and turned. The vibrant autumn shades she recalled from their last visit for the grape harvest were muted as colder weather set in. Leaves had fallen and fields were plowed into mounded rows. The gnarled stumps of the cutback vines offered a stark beauty against the bright blue sky and signaled the promise of the next year's bounty. Evergreen oaks, olive trees and cedars provided a backdrop of multi-hued greens.

Kat was eager to be back in the company of the people who had made her feel so welcome in June. She had come to know them so well.

Philippe phoned as soon as they turned off the main road, and when they arrived at the courtyard of the manoir, everyone was outside to deliver a boisterous welcome.

Joy; her daughter, Marie, and her son-in-law, Christian; her brother- and sister-in-law, Jean-Pierre and Madeleine Lallibert; Philippe's Oncle François; even the housekeeper/cooks Antoine and Hélène in their starched white aprons, were all there, as was, of course, Picasso, who bounded toward the car.

"Pico, Pico!" Katherine cried, kneeling to rub her face against the excited dog and wrapping her arms around his neck. The feel of his soft, golden hair gave her goosebumps. She loved the exuberant Lab and, for a moment, was overwhelmed by the bond she had forged with him months earlier. She held a thought before letting him go, although he did not leave her side: You taught me so much in a very short time, mon ami.

"I think his tail might just wag right off," Joy said as Kat stood to greet everyone, and they all laughed.

"We thought you were leaving us, ma chère. We are so excited and happy for you and Philippe to be together."

Joy offered apologies for the absence of her son, Henri, and his wife, Sylvie, who were hiking in Corsica. "Mirella sends their regrets as she and Marc are in Paris. She wanted you to know they share our happiness and look forward to seeing you at Christmas," she said, referring to her closest friends.

If I'm still here, Kat thought ruefully.

Joy led the way to sprawling terrace behind the manoir, where champagne was served, with foie gras spread on small toasts, and a selection of olives, and lively chatter filled the air.

Kat was embarrassed when she saw the bowls of olives. Joy grinned and touched her arm. "Philippe told me the story and that they were your new passion, so I could not resist."

The conversation turned serious when the topic of a local political situation came up. Philippe and Joy translated as needed and, in true Gallic fashion, the discussion ended in laughter as they made hilarious remarks about the people involved.

"The French always seems to find the humor in their politics, no matter what. It's a saving grace," Joy whispered to Kat.

Just then, Hélène appeared on the terrace to announce the meal was ready. A cool nip in the provençal air prevented their dining al fresco, and lunch was served in the massive banquet hall at a long table close to the fireplace. They shut the French doors to the terrace tightly behind them.

"It's our first daube de sanglier of the season. Just for you," Hélène whispered, her pride evident, as she set Kat's plate down.

Philippe discreetly leaned over and murmured, "Wild boar. Don't worry, it will be delicious."

The aromas of garlic and red wine floating up from her plate left Kat no doubt he was right.

"Christian and a party from the village were hunting last week and this was his quarry," Marie told Kat with evident pride.

The conversation turned to that expedition, with talk about the meal, which was part of the hunt tradition, they had eaten at mid-day at a small country inn.

"It always comes back to the food and wine, doesn't it?" Kat remarked to Joy, who simply smiled and nodded.

Conversation and laughter flew around the table. Oncle François' face was filled with happiness during the extended lunch, but he did not say much. Katherine looked forward to spending some quiet time with him. She was very fond of him and remembered her surprise when she had learned that this apparently simple goat herder was also a wealthy businessman. It had been a good lesson in not making snap judgments about people.

Kat was pleased with how well she could now follow the conversation and even participate in French. But there were still moments when one small error on her part brought it to a halt while everyone, laughing gently in support, tried to work out precisely what it was she meant. Kat laughed along with the rest. She had learned that having her mistakes corrected was an excellent way to learn the language.

At the end of the meal, coffee and a warm tarte aux pommes were served in the cozy salon.

François sat down by the roaring fire and, after catching Kat's attention, patted the chair next to him. She felt quite emotional as she bent to bise him. He took her hand, his lips lightly brushing its back. She was so fond of this kind, gentle man. He had changed her life in Paris in June with his advice that no one should hold back from deciding among the choices our short lives offer us.

"Eh bien, my beautiful Katherine, tell me all your joys. I believe my nephew is passionately in love with you, and if you love him the same way, you are making this old man très heureux."

Kat blushed, and François, smiling, lightly waved his trembling hand. They spoke quietly for some time until Joy joined them to say that a walk through the vineyard was being organized.

"Allez, ma chère. It's a fine day for a walk and time for my nap. We will see each other later."

Philippe joined them to tell Kat he would drive François home while she joined the others for the walk. "I'll stay with him for a while and see if there is anything I can do before I come back. He's doing well but he's still a bit fragile, as you can see."

He kissed her forehead. "I can see how happy you are to be back here."

She nodded, "It feels good—like family."

Katherine ran up to her room to change into her walking shoes. She was thankful for the heavy sweater she had purchased earlier in the week, and hoped the box of warm clothes would soon arrive that she had asked Molly to send. Joy had let her know in advance that a walk would probably be on the agenda, saying, "We take advantage of these cool autumn days before rain and mistral arrive. In the summer, it's often too hot or everyone is busy with something else. It will be perfect weather for a good hike when we are all together."

They set off at a brisk pace, walking through the vineyard and along a well-trodden path in the forest beyond.

Picasso led the way with enthusiasm whenever he wasn't over to the side investigating some intriguing scent.

Kat remarked to Joy that the landscape seemed calm compared to her previous visit, when everyone had been harvesting grapes and all the roads, big and small, had been buzzing with tractors and trucks delivering the crop to the wine co-ops.

"It is quieter here now, oui, but that doesn't mean the land is not busy," Joy said. "Olive harvesting begins soon and we all pitch in again, shaking the trees and raking the fruit that escape the nets. You will notice the nets we've placed under the trees when you drive back tomorrow, although some people still hang a basket around their necks and use ladders to pick the olives. Also, le ban des truffes, the truffle proclamation, will be announced in Richerenches next week and that's the start of truffle season. You must come with us to truffles market one weekend. It's such fun!"

Kat smiled. "There's still so much for me to learn about life here. I love all this, as you know."

"I'm glad you continue to find our lifestyle and traditions so pleasing. Who would have imagined you would trade your Canadian life for one here?"

"I still can't quite believe it, but every day the choices I have and the decisions I need to make are becoming clearer to me. It's scary in one way and thrilling in another."

"Life is all about choice, n'est-ce pas? I made a similar decision some sixty years ago when I left England and have never regretted my life in France. Sartre said, 'We are the choices we make.' I like that."

Katherine nodded and lapsed into silence. This past year had certainly opened up unimagined opportunities for choice.

After a few moments, Joy slowed their pace and in a quieter voice asked, "Has Philippe talked much about Geneviève's last years? Her illness? Her mother?"

Kat was surprised. She wasn't sure to what Joy was alluding. Even so, she felt uncomfortable.

"He mentioned there was something that he had to tell me," she said, searching Joy's face for a clue to what was meant.

Joy paused for a moment, deep in thought. "Attends, ma chère, all in good time. Don't worry, he will. I won't say more right now but we will talk once he has told you. I will be waiting for you to call me. Just know that."

Her look indicated that this was the end of that topic, and they hurried to catch up with the others. As they neared them, Joy put her arm around Kat. "I didn't mean to alarm you," she whispered, "There are things you need to know, c'est tout, and Philippe will tell you before long, trust me. Trust him."

Swallowing hard, Kat tried to set aside the anxiety that had bolted up in her. She told herself that it was still early days and they still had much to learn about each other. If Joy knew about the problem, it couldn't be that bad, could it?

Soon they were all chatting about local events and explaining to Kat some of the finer points of the truffle harvest. Everyone had a tale to tell. Kat tried her best to pay attention and to get past Joy's perplexing words.

The path the group followed through the woods eventually led to a gently rolling hillside that was an endless patchwork of olive groves and fields. There was still green to be seen but dried leaves crunched beneath their feet as they walked, evidence that the season was changing yet again.

Closing her eyes and breathing in deeply, Katherine caught the smell of wood smoke in the air. It was intoxicating. When she looked about her, she could see, here and there, trails of smoke floating skyward. It brought back memories of bonfires as a child, at her uncle's farm, and she told the others some stories about the countryside around St. Jacob's as they walked onward. They were all intrigued to learn a bit about Katherine's early life in Canada, and she felt a few tugs to her heart as she talked about that happy time.

Soon, over an hour had passed and they were walking past François' goatherd next to the Lallibert's farmhouse.

"I have such good memories of my exchange here," Katherine sighed, zipping up her jacket as the afternoon had begun to cool down quickly.

"That was the beginning of this French adventure for you," Joy said. Jean-Pierre and Madeleine beamed, as if they were responsible somehow for bringing Katherine to this point in her life. They said their goodbyes and laughed at Picasso's momentary confusion over whether to stay or keep going. When Katherine and Joy resumed walking, he bounded over to join them.

As they neared the manoir, they could see Philippe sitting on a bench in the courtyard, catching the last rays of sunshine.

"Eh bien, just in time for an apéritif."

They spent the evening lingering over dinner, immersed in quiet conversation. Kat found herself watching the two of them and wondered what secret it was that they shared. Was it her imagination, or was there really an edge to their attempts to appear relaxed? There were moments when she was certain they seemed ill at ease. She had also noticed them earlier, off to one side, talking. Still she wondered if she was reading more into the unknown than was necessary.

In the morning Joy packed them a basket of Hélène's still-warm croissants and pains au chocolat, fresh eggs and slices of Antoine's cured jambon.

When Joy said goodbye to Katherine, she hugged her and whispered, "Don't worry. Don't worry. I know it is not easy to wait, but Philippe is doing his best. I'll be here for you."

Kat's eyes filled with tears and she quickly wiped them away. "Thank you, " she whispered back. "I'll talk to you soon. It has to happen soon."

After bidding a fond au revoir to Picasso, they waved and called out "Merci mille fois" to Antoine and Hélène, who were leaning out the kitchen doors by the long driveway.

"Can you feel it?" Philippe asked, his voice husky.

Kat nodded, "It's almost as if we were there to receive blessings from Joy and François."

Philippe agreed with a smile, saying he had not seen his uncle so at peace in a very long time. There was a long silence before Katherine responded.

"Being here is always such a happy time for me, but I'm not feeling at peace now" she said, choosing her words carefully. "I can't wait much longer for you to be straight with me. You need to know that. It's not fair. I've explained to you before how I feel about our being honest with each other. It's essential to me, and you had me believing it was to you as well."

"It is. You know it is," he said. "I'm not being dishonest. I just haven't told you everything. I can't yet, but I promise I will."

Kat shook her head. "I'm running out of patience. It's got to be soon."

Neither of them spoke for a while, then Philippe said, "You have no idea how hard I am working to make this problem go away. If it doesn't, you may want to leave, and that is my greatest fear. But it also may be the best thing for you."

Kat was shocked, and it took her a minute to respond. "Don't you understand how awful it is for me to hear you say that? For you to suggest I might walk away from our life together? I can't imagine what you are thinking."

Philippe nodded solemnly, his eyes fixed straight ahead. "Just a little longer, Kat, just a little longer. Fais-moi confiance. Trust me."

She sighed heavily and looked out the window, thinking that she must be crazy to accept his assurance, or at least crazy in love. He was right though. He was being honest. She just had to wait until he fixed whatever it was that was broken.

She settled back in her seat and tried to sleep.

8

Kat emailed Molly and Andrea as soon as she arrived home that evening. To her surprise Molly Skyped her first thing the next morning.

"What are you doing home?"

Molly squeaked out a response. "Laryngitis. It's flu season here again."

"Oh no! Why don't you call me when you feel better?"

Molly shook her head. "I'll just whisper. You talk. Sounds like you need to."

Kat filled her in.

"Trouble in paradise," was Molly's first comment.

Kat ran her hands through her hair, her frustration showing.

"Katski, don't get bent out of shape about this. It could be something relatively simple."

"Well, it seems to be a bit more than that. Obviously there are others involved, or at least know about whatever it is."

"Yeah, whateverthefu–. I mean, whateverthefrickitis. Sorry, still working on that," Molly rasped. "You said Philippe has mentioned a few times that he has something he needs to tell you."

"When the time is right, is what he keeps saying. Sometimes I can forget about it, but other times it makes me crazy. On the way back from Sainte Mathilde, I kind of lost it."

Molly was silent. Then she blew her nose and cleared her throat. "The good news is that he isn't trying to hide anything. He's just sifting through some sort of shit before he can explain it to you. Trust him. He's been so good to you in every other way."

Kat sighed, long and hard. "You're right. He's sweet, loving, fun, kind and all the things I never knew were missing in my life. We talk about everything, so I hadn't pegged him as someone to keep secrets from me."

"He's just stalling. You need to trust him."

"Trust. I've been thinking about that all night. It sounds kind of crazy but trust is something I never really thought about until James left me."

"That's the thing, my friend. Trust isn't an issue until you have been deceived. After that, it moves right up the ladder to hang with love and respect. Trust me—I couldn't resist that—with my history of failed expectations, I know. You know I know."

Kat nodded. Molly did indeed know about deception. She had lived with it through all of her dysfunctional childhood.

"Should we stop talking? How are you feeling?"

"I'm not finished with my two cents' worth yet, my friend."

"Tell me when you need to stop."

"Listen, Kat, you had such a grounded life. No one let you down until you were fifty-five."

"And I remember clearly you telling me, after James left, that trust takes only seconds to break and forever to rebuild. Now, I feel like trust is something I need to believe in. It's a strange mindset for me. I don't want to be suspicious of Philippe."

"But remember, we were talking about trust and James. He deceived you in the worst way, and it would be very difficult to trust him again. Philippe isn't deceiving you. He's asking you to wait till he sorts something out. That's very different."

Both women sat quietly for a few seconds, looking at each other. Then Molly cocked her head and gave Kat a wide-eyed look that demanded a response.

"Thanks, Moll. You are right. That was about James, and this isn't."

Molly nodded, waiting for more.

"It's so helpful to talk to you about this," Kat continued. "I feel better already. I do believe in Philippe. I'll wait for him to find the right moment to tell me what this is all about."

"Atta girl! Now tell me more about everything else. What's happening with your photography? Are you still thinking about committing to it full time?"

"I'm a little nervous about it."

"Those photos you sent from that town, Antrawhatsit –"

"Entrevaux"

"Sheesh. Pardon my French. Well, they were outstanding. What a fascinating place, and so different from the coast."

"Thanks. I'm glad you liked them. Google the history of the area, Moll, you'll find it intriguing. Honestly, this country continues to amaze me. Blah, blah, blah, there I go again."

"Oh you do go on about France, and I love it but I'm beginning to fade. I think I need to lie down for a while. Are you good now?"

"I'm feeling better. Thanks for being you."

Later that morning, Andrea called, and their conversation brought Kat to the same place, although via a different route. The cousins' lives had mirrored each other's in that they had grown up in loving, stable families, which encouraged them to achieve and believe in themselves. They had both been in long marriages.

"Until mine blew up in my face," Kat said.

"A hurt that will have a lasting impact," Andrea said. "But then, look at the good that has come into your life now. You took a chance and—wow! I agree with everything Molly said. Don't judge Philippe based on your experience with James."

Kat was soon pouring her heart out to her cousin.

"Most of the time everything is great and we truly feel like a couple. We're happy with each other in every small way, and our passion is strong and deep."

"And the problem is?"

"I can't stop thinking about the fact that he is keeping a secret from me."

"But he said he would tell you what it is when the time is right."

"I know. I'm not certain I can wait any longer. I've opened my heart to him in every way, and now I'm suddenly feeling afraid. In true love there can be no secrets."

"I agree, but this is a little different."

Kat was quiet for a few seconds. "A secret is a secret. It means you're hiding something, and when you do that you compromise your relationship. I just never expected Philippe to do something like that." Her voice became tight. She was close to tears. "And now I'm afraid I don't know him as well as I thought. It's all about trust. How can I trust him?"

Andrea spoke slowly and with great care. "Kat, I understand where you're coming from but I think you need to keep your composure. Keep believing in what you do know about him. It sounds like he's trying to protect you, not deceive you."

"I know, I know. We've had this conversation before, but it's really beginning to bother me, obviously."

"Kat, you told me before you were willing to wait until after Christmas. Do that, and keep trusting the love you were feeling last night. Go to yoga and clear your head."

Kat nodded. "I'm so blessed to have you in my life."

"Me more!"

One thing Kat and Philippe never ran out of was conversation. They laughed at times, saying they had obviously been storing it for years. For Kat, it was a refreshing change from the long periods of silence she had endured during her marriage. More and more, their conversation switched back and forth between French and English.

She was often frustrated by the mistakes she made, and Philippe would gently correct them and praise her improving skill. Other times they fell about, laughing at some major blooper. Her friend, Annette, was also very patient and they agreed some days just to speak French to each other. It all helped.

She knew it would take time to become proficient in French and was pleased to have found Ida, a language instructor, whom she met in a café across the street a few times a week. It was a casual arrangement, at times that worked for both of them, and the instruction was entirely in French.

Ida spoke perfectly articulated Parisian French that was a pleasure to hear. She would have Katherine read a newspaper article, and they would discuss the details and vocabulary. That inevitably led to a chat about this and that.

Parisian-born, Ida was candid about the difficulties in learning a foreign language. "It's not simply a matter of vocabulary, grammar and syntax. Culture and history affect language in subtle ways, too. In double entendres, for instance, that are almost impossible to learn. Don't let it deter you; it's something you will have to accept."

Kat hoped she could do just that and counted herself lucky in having an instructor who looked at the big picture and didn't focus solely on grammar and vocabulary.

"There are times when I just can't work my way around certain words. The letters seem to get stuck in my mouth."

Ida laughed. "C'est une forme de gymnastique quelquefois—verbal gymnastics. That's often what speaking French feels like."

"That's the perfect description for those moments," Kat said

"Then at other times it all comes together and it's smooth and easy—une ballade dans la bouche—a song in your mouth."

Kat's face lit up. "I love speaking this language, even when I know I'm making mistakes."

"And that's why you will do just fine," Ida said. "The love of the language is half the battle."

9

The market was closed on Mondays through the winter, but Philippe had a busy day planned. The investigators from Nice had emailed to say they would be at the fire site to meet with him early in the morning. He expected to hear that they had finished examining the storage unit, and so he had arranged for him and Gilles, with other friends helping, to install new shelving and refrigeration in the unit that afternoon. Then they could move their stock back into it.

Kat planned a full day on the Cap to work in the garden there. Massive flowerbeds, overgrown and untamed, were beginning to show the results of the care and hard labor she and Philippe had put into trimming everything back and rooting out the weeds. They were beginning to slowly replace missing shrubs and vines, using old photos and paintings of the property that had been saved, some carefully and some accidentally.

It still astonished her that this stunning property, with its panoramic views across the sea to the old town of Antibes and over the Baie des Anges to Nice and the hills beyond, had been abandoned for decades. Left to fall into ruin, hidden behind thick hedges and now-crumbling walls, it was the victim of a long-simmering family feud. Philippe told her that after his grandfather's death, two branches of his family had fought over the archaic inheritance laws and legal details that had not been properly addressed. By the time the issues were settled, and Philippe was named the legal heir, his wife, Geneviève, had become terminally ill.

The villa, close to derelict when Philippe first took Katherine to see it, was now the focus of their dream of building a future here. That vision was evolving into a detailed restoration plan almost complete on paper and ready to commence as soon as possible. In the meantime, they continued to attack the overgrown gardens.

Philippe's days began early, so late nights for him were rare. But still, they had stayed awake on several nights, exchanging and refining their ideas on how to turn the villa into the small inn they would open one day. It was a fantasy they were determined to make happen.

In some ways, the evolution of this land and the storied villa reflected the growth of the bond between the two lovers. Their pledge to the project and to each other grew stronger as the days passed. Their friendship had been a few months. Their courtship, a few weeks. Their love felt like it would last forever.

If only Philippe would tell her his secrets. Despite Molly and Andrea's advice, Kat was still feeling hurt that Philippe was keeping something important from her.

On her way to the Cap property this morning, Kat paused to shoot a close-up photo of a cluster of unusual mushrooms growing by the roadside. A rich, caramel color with delicate rust-colored gills and silky beige stems, the mushrooms were the largest she had ever seen.

She had once jokingly told Philippe she thought she could put together a photo book only about mushrooms in France. The vendor's stall at the market in Nice, which constantly displayed exotic-looking varieties, was a favorite spot for her to shoot. It was there that she witnessed customers ask for a mushroom to be cut open for them to inspect before buying. She had never seen that happen before.

Philippe told her how he and other friends would often go into the countryside during the short mushroom season.

"The peak time is from mid-August to mid-September," he said. "We pick only on public property and most of us guard our secret places. C'est vrai! We don't want anyone to know."

He explained how they would set up a grill to cook the freshly picked bounty right where they had found it. "Can't get any fresher than that. We will go next year."

He had also told her of the number of fatal accidents that occur because many varieties are poisonous. "You can take your basket of mushrooms into almost any pharmacy and they will be able to tell you whether yours are edible. Most French mushroom-lovers are well educated about them, but accidents do happen."

"Mushrooms are definitely an art here," she mentioned to Andrea one day on Skype. "I basically thought that if you've tasted one mushroom, you've tasted them all. I thought they were all like the portobello and those little button ones. I mean, even I knew those. But they are just the tip of the iceberg."

Andrea had laughed. She ran an organic farm, so she knew a lot about mushrooms. "When Terrence and I visit you the next time we'll spend a lot more time at the markets. I want to take a look at those fungi."

Now, as Kat stepped closer to the mushrooms in the ditch, adjusting her camera lens, she became aware of a faint snuffling coming from behind the tall hedge. When she heard it again, she carefully picked her way through the ditch to peer between the bushes.

She jumped back in surprise, swallowing a squeal, as a pair of deep dark eyes rimmed by long, thick lashes, peered back. A mottled coat of varied shades of gray mixed with white came into view, followed by the creature's square-jawed head, which sported two enormous ears separated by a thick black Mohawk-like mane. The animal emitted a loud, nasal, bray.

An old donkey, only slightly disheveled, was staring at her through the bushes and twitching its ears at the flies buzzing around.

She reached her hand across the wire fence behind the hedge and held it there for the dappled critter to sniff. After a moment, a silky, moist nose shyly and hesitantly nuzzled her fingers. After pulling back a few times and then quickly returning, it allowed her to lightly rub its velvety muzzle. There was an inquisitive look in its eyes that seemed to invite more communication.

Kat had been holding her breath but she slowly realized the air held only a hint of an offensive smell. This was a well-cared-for animal.

"Salut, little fellow. Petit ami." She snapped a few shots, zooming in on the coarse texture of its coat, as the donkey slowly backed away and calmly began grazing.

"Parlez-vous anglais ou français?" she asked with a grin.

She could see no sign of anyone as she leaned through the hedge to look at the property. Beyond the paddock where the donkey stood, she could see a garden that appeared moderately well cared for and, beyond it, a somewhat neglected-looking cottage that seemed to be inhabited. Its shutters were open and a few items of clothing hung on a line.

Philippe was surprised when she told him about it that evening and said, "Un petit âne? I thought that property was abandoned like mine."

"The donkey seems well fed and surprisingly clean, and it's not very smelly, either. So someone obviously is there caring for it. But the place feels kind of mysterious. I may try to find out more about it one of these days."

He gave her a nudge and grinned. "There you go, Minou, starting another adventure and discovering things around you that most of us simply pass by."

She had to admit this seemed to be part of her new persona. It made her wonder how she could ever have been happy, so confined in her marriage for all those years. Why had she never considered making a change? Why had she simply turned a blind eye to James's controlling ways, like a battered wife, and carried on? Better the devil you know. How often had she said that to herself?

At the time, she thought she was content, that their marriage was how things were supposed to be, even as she felt her spirit weakened by his bullying. It had seemed easier to stay than to go. Now she knew just how wrong she had been all those years. Philippe had shown her how it feels to be truly loved. But if he loved her, how could he keep this secret from her? This "WTF' situation, as Molly called it, was serious. Kat felt her impatience flare again—to get it out in the open, get it resolved and get back to where they were before he ever found that note tucked under the wiper.

10

Katherine was startled when Philippe walked in from work the next afternoon, clearly agitated and angry. This was the second time in a few weeks she had witnessed this uncharacteristic behavior, the first being when the SUV had tried to force them off the road on the way to Entrevaux.

"The investigators from Nice were back again this morning with their portable lab. They wanted to confirm some findings they reached over the weekend. They arrived at a different conclusion than the local police. Apparently the blast was deliberately set and had nothing to do with the electrical wiring in the storage area. They found traces of plastic explosives that could only have been left by a handmade device."

Kat was shocked. "But who would do this on purpose?" she asked. "And why would they, for heaven's sake? Competitors? Surely not!"

Philippe shook his head. "Malheureusement, I have a very good idea," he said.

Then the light went on for Katherine. "Mon Dieu! Tell me this isn't connected to your problem, please."

"I have to think it is," he said. "But it could turn out to be a good thing because some incriminating evidence was left. It's being checked out now in Nice and may be sent to Paris. I had to tell them about the note and the threats."

Katherine was perplexed. She stared at him. "Threats? Plural?"

He nodded sheepishly and looked away.

Kat waited till he looked back. Her gaze was unwavering. "I've been good about trying to put this out of my mind. In fact, I had almost convinced myself that the car chase was a case of mistaken identity. I really had. But this is something else again. You have to tell me what's going on."

"Soon. I promise."

There was a long silence between them. There was nothing more either of them could say. Then Philippe's phone rang and he left the room.

Kat put on some warm biking clothes and headed out on her own. She needed time to work through this—again. She wasn't certain she could. Keeping secrets held hurtful memories for her, and she thought she had made that clear to him, more than once.

"I'm going for a ride. Back in an hour or so," she called as she opened the front door.

She heard him say goodbye on the phone and then he called back, "Attends-moi! Wait a few minutes and I'll go with you."

"To be honest, I want to be alone."

She took one of her favorite routes across the Cap and through a few back streets until suddenly she was riding through the quiet forest. For the first while she let the rhythm of her movement calm her and focused only on that. Then she pulled her bike up against a stone wall and climbed up a short slope to a small clearing that gave her a clear view down to the sea.

This was the vista she loved most and had seen from so many vantage points on the rides they had taken. She felt it belonged just to her. It was part of why she was so in love with the Côte d'Azur. At this moment she was searching for something from it—peace, strength, guidance? Something.

For the first time since that fateful night at the airport, she was feeling unsure of herself. Questions that had been nagging her for days raised themselves again, and she knew she had to answer them. She closed her eyes while she thought them through.

Was she where she truly belonged? She thought she was.

Could she completely change her life like this? She thought she could.

Were six months enough time to know everything she needed to about Philippe? Apparently not.

Should this worry her? This was the stumbling block. She had once thought she knew everything about James and had been blindsided after twenty-two years.

Now Philippe was keeping something from her. Why? What? It frightened her, and it hurt her that he would not tell her what it was.

Should she confront him? No. Their relationship ruled out confrontation. He had asked her to give him time, so maybe she should. Molly and Andrea thought so. It's not like he was denying there was something. He just needed time. She still needed time.

Opening her eyes now, she gave herself over completely to the beauty of the land and sea spread out before her, and all that it represented to her. She loved this view. She loved this country. She loved Philippe.

Then she got back on her bike.

No. No more time.

She needed the wait to be over.

11

Dusk was falling when Kat got back to the apartment. Philippe was quickly at the door to put his arms around her.

"I was getting worried. I tried your cell, but you must have forgotten it and that's not like you."

"No, I had it with me. I just didn't feel like answering it," she told him as she hung up her jacket and turned to face him.

Alarmed by her answer, Philippe moved toward her once more but stopped when he saw her expression.

Kat was anchored to where she stood, her face tight with emotion. She clenched her hands. She didn't want to, but she felt herself losing control.

Philippe's smile froze. "What is it?"

"I can't pretend any longer..." She paused before a torrent of words poured out. "I'm almost paralyzed with fear that something terrible is going to happen between us. You must tell me, immediately, what this secret is of yours. Something is going on, and I can't wait any longer."

Philippe reached for her hand and led her to the couch in the salon. He sat facing her, his face solemn, and closed his eyes for a moment before he spoke.

"You're right. I can't keep this from you any more. I thought I could, but it is a bigger problem than I first imagined."

Katherine's heart started to pound.

"It goes back to when I first met Geneviève, or Vivi, Viv, as she preferred. We were young and wild and ..." He paused, swallowing hard, his eyes downcast. Then he raised his head and looked out through the dark window. "She was an addict, a product of a very rough background. Her mother lived with a Russian drug dealer. He was not Viv's father, but he was around a lot. He was very controlling. He never took drugs himself, and when he found out Vivi was hooked, he threw her out."

Kat sat quietly still holding Philippe's hand. She felt awkward and unsure how to comfort him.

"They lived in the north, in Britanny, and Viv ran away to Cannes. I met her at a party and at first we were just friends in a large group of crazy young people living life as you do at that age. But soon I realized she had a problem. Another friend, Maurice—sadly he is no longer alive—but Maurice and I eventually got her into rehab, and we were her support when she was discharged. After a year, she and I became lovers and were soon married. She had no contact with her mother. Viv was a warm, loving woman but she harbored great bitterness toward her mother. She felt she had been abandoned for the Russian."

Kat nodded, her eyes sympathetic.

"She went to school, a business school, and studied very hard to become an accountant. Imagine! From one extreme to another. And she was very good at what she did." His voice cracked with emotion, and he shook his head.

"Two years later Adorée was born and life was fine until Viv became sick with cancer, an aggressive strain of leukemia, when Adorée was fifteen."

"I'm so sorry."

"That's when everything fell apart. Her mother, Idelle, suddenly contacted us. She had always known where Viv was but she had wisely stayed out of our lives. Her sister was Denise's mother. Denise is a cousin who lives in Lyon, and she was passing on our news, although at the time we had no idea."

Kat's mouth was dry. Her mind was filled with confusion, but she listened patiently.

"Idelle had never stopped loving Viv, but she was under Dimitri's spell until she heard about her illness. That trumped everything. Now Idelle researched every available treatment for this type of cancer and wanted to take Viv to a special clinic in Germany. Viv resisted her urging for a year and went through a chemo program. It was brutal, but she did it with such grace. She wanted to be brave for Adorée, who was everything to her."

He paused again. Kat could feel his anguish and drew him into her arms. He held her close and buried his face in her shoulder. "You don't have to continue now if you don't want to," she whispered.

His reply was muffled. "Yes. I do. I need to tell you the whole story now I have started."

"Let me get us some water then."

Philippe drew back. "Non," he said, "there's an open bottle of Cabernet on the counter. Let's have that."

He stood and stretched, running his hands through his hair, as she left the room.

When she returned, he was at the window looking down to the sea. They stood together for a while, sipping the wine. Kat lightly rubbed his back as he continued.

"Three months later the doctors told us there was nothing more they could do. The cancer had returned with a vengeance. They said it would only be a matter of months before she passed. Idelle was on our doorstep within days, and you can imagine the mix of emotions that filled the air. Viv asked me to leave them alone for a while and I did. I didn't want to, but I let them talk alone."

He began pacing the room. Kat sat back down on the couch.

"I am going to skip a lot of details and get to the—as you say—the line at the bottom."

Kat let that go.

"Viv was desperate to stay alive, and Idelle convinced her she could make that happen. Honnêtement, I believed that all Idelle wanted was to save her daughter. I still do."

He took a long sip of wine and nodded slowly, his lips a grim line.

"She insisted that she had never stopped loving Viv and had always regretted that she hadn't defended her from Dimitri so long ago. She said she felt it was best to stay out of our lives because she too had become addicted—to methamphetamines—but Dimitri accepted it. That drug had become his specialty, and she was his guinea pig. She knew Viv was safer away from them, as his whole business became busier and more dangerous." Philippe's voice was shaking with emotion.

"I should have known better, but we were all so desperate. You can't imagine how your mind works when the person you love is about to die. It's not like the terrible suddenness of a car accident or a heart attack. You have to look death in the face every day, and the feeling of helplessness is something I cannot begin to describe. No matter how much you hope and pray for a miracle, you can't get away from the reality. It pokes you and prods you. It's like sitting on a time bomb. Tick, tick, tick ..." His voice trailed off.

Kat's eyes filled with tears, and she waited quietly for him to speak again.

"I admire people who have a strong faith. It gives them such grace to accept death. But that wasn't us. Viv went to Germany for a month with Idelle. The treatment seemed to help, but the side effects were extremely painful. They returned to Antibes for a month and then went back to Germany for another six weeks. Her behavior was a bit odd while they were here, but I put it down to her treatment."

He drained the wine from his glass.

Wiping tears from her face, Kat left to get the rest of the bottle. Philippe followed her into the kitchen and continued the story.

"What you must know is that Adorée never knew about her mother's past involvement with drugs, and she thought her grandparents had passed away when she was a baby. So when Idelle appeared on the scene, we simply said she was a friend of Tante Céleste in Lyon. Viv did not show great affection for Idelle anyway, so it seemed believable." He motioned to Kat to sit at the kitchen table with him.

"Three weeks into the treatment in Germany, I went to visit. I arrived much sooner than expected as I was able to get on an earlier flight. Viv was startled to see me when the clinic receptionist called her to the waiting area, but she was upbeat and happy, which surprised me. There were other people around, and we simply bised before we went up to her small suite. The clinic was beautiful—very modern and well-appointed in that clean, Germanic style."

Kat wondered where he was going with the story, as he spoke on about the furnishings, artwork, and the size of his wife's accommodation, until it occurred to her he was stalling. She said nothing. A minute or two later, he stopped talking and drained his glass. Then he inhaled deeply, and resumed the story, his voice shaking with anger.

"When we got to her room, I took her in my arms and we embraced again and again. Then we kissed. Her lips were dry and tasted bitter and I pulled back when my tongue started to tingle sharply. She turned away for a moment and then looked back at me with a frightening determination." He spoke rapidly now, his voice still low.

"She said she was taking cocaine. That it was not interfering with the treatment and was the only thing that made her feel better. She thought that, as she was dying, the drugs were not an issue. Then she shocked me even more by saying that she was going to keep taking it when she came home. She promised to hide it, and that Adorée would never know."

He began pacing again, his fists clenched. "I will never forget the pain in her voice. The desperation ..." He squeezed his eyes shut as he struggled to control his emotions.

"What is the answer to that?" he said, his voice rising with anger and anguish. "Dis-moi! Someone you love is dying, and the only thing that helps her feel human is an illegal drug. What the hell do you do? Deprive her of a warped sense of peace in her final days?" He sat down and wept silently into his hands, his shoulders shaking. Before Kat could go to him, he wiped his eyes, stood and started pacing again.

"The moral conflict might have been intolerable, but at that moment I didn't care. I just wanted her to live—to feel alive. I would have died so she could live. Anything ..."

Kat reached for a tissue to wipe her eyes. Philippe dropped into his chair, as if all the anger had suddenly escaped him. They sat in silence for several minutes, before he wiped his face with his hands. "I'm sorry, Minou. I didn't mean to unload all of this on you. I have kept it buried for years."

She moved behind him and gently massaged his shoulders. "Perhaps it's time it all came out, and you begin to let go of it. I'm here for you."

Philippe reached back and clasped her hands, tenderly squeezing them.

"It was Idelle who left that note under the wiper, the day we went to Entrevaux. It's brought all of this to the surface for me. These memories have been tormenting me, but you, being the woman you are and offering me the love that you do, have let me unlock them."

Kat, her hands still on his shoulders, leaned down to kiss his cheek. She felt his back straighten and become strong again. He cleared his voice.

"I mean, what she did for Viv is not normal. Who does something like that? But for someone like Idelle it was an obvious solution. She was giving her daughter an escape from pain and worry. But it didn't stop there."

He stood again and paced as he spoke, after a very long sigh.

"What I haven't mentioned was the cost of the cocaine. At first Idelle provided it for nothing, but as time went by she demanded payment, blaming Dimitri. This was the purest form of the drug and expensive beyond words, and as Viv's pain increased, she needed more of it. The debt became unmanageable. It never occurred to me that this was part of Dimitri's plan."

Kat's head was spinning. This was like nothing she could have imagined.

"At some point Viv mentioned to Idelle that at long last the legal issues over the property on the Cap had been settled in our favor. I did not find this out until after Viv died—and she lived for another ten months. I knew it was the drugs that allowed her to be present for Adorée—and to have fun with her, often. It was torture for me, but she continued to live in her own little bubble. Tante Idelle visited regularly with the supply. I felt like a prisoner myself, trapped. I wanted to protect Adorée while trying to say goodbye to Viv and help her die with dignity."

"I can't imagine how hard it was for you," Kat murmured.

"After Viv died, Idelle came to me with a deal. She would forgive the debt and promised that Adorée would never know of her mother's drug history, if I would agree to allow Dimitri access to a hidden cove at the foot of our property. When I refused, and told her I would pay the debt somehow, it became a blackmail threat. Do it or Adorée and the public will know about Viv's drug use—past and present. They would say I was supplying them to Viv and others. These are nasty people, I promise you."

"Obviously," Kat agreed.

"I was distraught, not thinking properly. I just wanted that woman out of our lives." Philippe let out a long, low sigh. "I wanted to forget the previous two years, and yet at the same time I needed to let go of my wife and remember the good things about her and about our life together. I had to deal with the grief and the anger that comes with a normal loss, let alone the complications involved morally and emotionally by her addiction. I thought I was going to go crazy."

Going back to the window, he stared out into the darkness that had fallen. "I thought I would never go back to the property again. It was a dream that just would not happen. I would leave it to Adorée to inherit, by which time these criminals hopefully would be long gone. So eventually I agreed."

He stopped in the middle of the room, his shoulders hunched and his arms hanging at his sides, and looked at Kat. "That's the story … in all of its ugliness."

Then he slumped into a chair, holding his head in his hands.

They sat for a while before she reached across and took his hand. Their eyes met.

"I don't know what to say except I am so sorry—for all of you. This is not how life should be—or death ..."

Philippe slowly lifted his head and straightened up.

"Well, Idelle is back. That's what the note was about."

"But what trouble can she cause now?"

"She knows we are fixing up the property. Whatever they use the cove for—and if I am honest I know it is to bring in drugs—they think they are going to lose their access. And they are right. I have more than paid my debt. They have used it for seven years, and I have closed my eyes. It has tormented me, but I will do anything to protect Adorée from the truth. She idolized her mother."

"So you can't tell this to the police investigating the fire?"

"I have to be careful what law enforcement I involve. These are immoral, insensitive criminals, who would just as soon shoot us as not. I'm afraid of what they might do if they find out I have contacted the police. En réalité, we could all be at risk."

Kat stared at him in disbelief. "Come on."

"I'm serious. I know it sounds like a low-budget movie, but it is real. Whoever was in the SUV that tried to drive us off the road to Entrevaux, was sent by them, I am sure of that. They are dangerous people. The simple solution is to leave the property as it is and walk away from our dream."

"That's just not right. You are giving in to blackmail. Somehow the police need to know about this, don't they?"

"I trust all of our local gendarmes. I've known most of them for a very long time. But this goes way beyond them. The department in Nice investigating the fire turned their findings over to the drug enforcement division in Paris."

Kat looked puzzled. "And that's not a good thing?"

"Definitely not. That's where you can't tell the good guys from the bad. The drug industry can buy anyone. There is so much corruption everywhere; I fear Dimitri may find out and we could all be in danger."

Shivers ran up Kat's spine. "I ... I ... don't know what to say."

"Minou, I am so sorry you had to know any of this. I am so sorry I have put you at risk. I understand if you want to leave. This is not what our life together promised."

Kat struggled for a response. "This is just so unreal. It sounds like a cable TV series."

"Quoi? A what?"

"Sorry. That was an insensitive comment. There's a saying that sometimes life is stranger than fiction, and this certainly is that. This is about the woman you loved. Does anyone else know?"

Philippe shook his head. "Joy and François know about the problems when Viv was sick. They know about her initial addiction when we first met and then what happened when she went with Idelle for treatment. I have told Joy about these threats, but not François. He doesn't need this to worry about. We all thought Idelle was out of our lives."

"We can't solve this by ourselves."

Philippe looked at her. "We? Are you certain you want to get involved?"

"Do I want to be involved in something like this? Non. Will I walk away from you and the promise of our life together because of it? Non, encore."

Philippe looked at her with surprise, as if he had not counted on this reaction from her.

"I love you, Philippe. I want to spend my life with you. I will not let this come between us." Her voice cracked and her jaw quivered as she fought to hold off tears again.

Philippe opened his arms to her, and they clung to each other. Then he pulled back a little and stared into her eyes, saying, "I love you too, Minou. I should never have doubted that you would stay with me—that you would want to help me."

Kat recovered her voice. "This is bigger than us. We need help. We need the police."

"I agree we need help. I'm just worried about where to look for it."

They sat back down and were silent for several minutes, lost in thought.

Kat struggled to sort through all she was hearing. On the one hand, her life had turned into a dream come true these past few months and, on the other, she was now caught up in a terrible mess. It was difficult to compute but she also knew there had to be a way out of the latter. Whatever the case, she had no doubt they were in it together.

"I wonder what Nick did? What police worked on that case?" Kat wondered out loud. "That was all drug-related too and he got pulled in as an innocent bystander. Right?"

Nick was an Australian bon vivant they had both known during the summer. He usually lived on his enormous luxury yacht in Antibes' Port Vauban, but had left abruptly the previous summer. At that time, he cut off all contact as he knew his phone would be bugged and wished to implicate no one. Even though they heard he was finally proved innocent, he had not returned to Antibes.

Philippe stood suddenly and walked over to his computer. "That's a thought. At least it's a place to start. I've got contact information from Tim somewhere here."

Tim was the captain of Nick's yacht and Kat agreed that if anyone would know how to find Nick, he would.

Philippe's eyes squinted in concentration as he two-finger typed. "Ah bon! Here's Tim's email. I'll send a message this minute."

Kat sighed. "That was a very intense hour. I feel drained and I can only imagine how you feel."

"I feel the same, but I'm also relieved that you know everything. Keeping this from you was agonizing. I just wanted it to go away and not be part of our life together."

"If I said I can't believe this is happening, it would be an understatement. But that's life, isn't it? There's always something ... maybe not usually something like this though." Kat shook her head in exasperation. "My mother often reminded me what doesn't kill us makes us stronger. I'm hearing those words loud and clear right now."

They stood quietly at the window, seeing nothing.

Philippe spoke first. "Let's go for a walk by the sea. La Grande Bleue always is a comfort, even on days like this. Bundle up warmly, and we'll stop for an espresso. Tomorrow we will make a plan."

12

Kat's eyes flew open and she sat straight up in bed. She'd been wakened by a loud, unearthly roar outside. In the darkness, she reached for Philippe and was even more alarmed to find he wasn't there. Now she was gripped with fear.

Shouting his name over the clamor, she switched on the light beside the bed and got to her feet. Sleep had been fleeting at best that night, with everything they had talked about on their minds.

They collided in the doorway.

"What's that noise?" she asked, her voice filled with panic. "It sounds like the world is coming to an end."

Laughing as he hugged her, Philippe said, "Minou, I would like to introduce you to le mistral. You are finally experiencing your first, and it's going to be a big one, according to la météo. I was checking that the shutters were all shut tight."

"It sounds like a locomotive roaring down the lane!"

"There's no mistaking it. I should have warned you when the temperature dropped so dramatically yesterday, but we were distracted, to say the least. We are used to it here and, truthfully, they don't happen that often on the coast. Our back alley is like a funnel and makes it sounds louder than it really is."

Relieved, Kat reached for her robe. "After the recent events and our talk yesterday, I thought we were under attack. Seriously."

"I don't blame you, but it's just the wind, a very big wind," he assured her.

"I won't be able to get back to sleep with this racket. It's almost five. Shall I make us some breakfast for a change?"

While she cooked, Philippe told her about the famous wind—"Mi-ange, mi-démon de la Provence—half-angel, half-devil"—that was in some ways welcomed by the people of Provence.

"The cold air piles up in the Alps and then rushes down along the valleys to us," he explained. "That's why the trees are all bent in one direction farther along the coast. Through the Var and the Bouches du Rhône, it's the worst. Marseille and Saint-Tropez get the full brunt of it as the cold air hits the sea."

Kat shuddered. "I can't imagine how it could be worse than this!"

"Extreme mistrals devastate crops and cause a lot of damage to exposed farmlands. Joy can tell some tales. But, as cold and fierce as it is, the wind blows away the dust in the air that comes to us from Africa and brings back our famous blue skies. There's a saying: 'Beauty comes after the wind.'"

Kat served them her special poached eggs, sprinkled with feta cheese and fresh mint, and as they ate, they returned to the problem they were facing. They were both amazed at how calmly they could talk about it, now that it was out in the open.

"It doesn't seem real," Kat said, shaking her head in wonder. "It feels like we're working out someone else's problem. Honestly, I'm not at all afraid, right now anyway. I still can't believe it."

"It's real, and you can see my reaction is pure anger."

They decided they should wait to hear what the special investigation revealed when Philippe met with the officers from Paris, a meeting that would happen by week's end. He checked his email, hoping to discover Nick did have connections in high places after being tangled in a drug-related investigation.

Tim's email response was there with a phone number and Philippe placed a call now that went straight to voicemail. Philippe grinned and passed the phone so Kat could hear the chirpy British accent of Tim's wife, Twig, on the recording. The sound of her friendly voice cheered them both. Tim and Twig had become friends of theirs before they left

Antibes on Nick's yacht. As far as anyone knew, they had docked it somewhere along the coast of north Africa.

Philippe left a message asking for either Tim or Nick to call back urgently at the number on this new phone, which they had purchased the night before.

"I'm going to sound completely paranoid," Philippe had said while they were out walking then, "but I don't think it's a good idea to use either of our phones. This cheap throwaway model should serve the purpose."

"I think you are being smart, not paranoid," Kat said.

As he prepared to leave for work now, she expressed her amazement that the market would even be open in the storm.

"Bien sûr! We'll drop the plastic flaps, batten them down and carry on. I doubt we will be busy though."

"Business as usual seems to be the norm in France, no matter what."

"It is. And we're going to attempt to live our lives as usual too while we wait for things to unfold. That explosion was meant to frighten us—and it did—but it could have been much, much worse. They're not desperate yet. I think we have some time. But please, Kat, for now, don't talk about this to anyone. Not even Andrea and Molly. Who knows who might be listening."

13

A day later, the wind had died down, as Philippe promised. The sky was once again its familiar, stunning blue as Kat walked to the property on the Cap.

Before she left, she tucked an apple into her pocket, and now she stopped to feed it to the donkey, which she had decided to name Eeyore. She cleared the growth in the ditch and leaned through the hedge. She could see him standing halfway up the hill. She knew he saw her, but he was not budging. Then he suddenly brayed.

Katherine made clucking noises. "Viens, Eeyore. Viens. Come." Holding the apple flat on her palm, she slowly waved her arm back and forth.

Eeyore brayed again and again, but he still refused to move.

Kat had a flashback to the farmhouse in Provence. Picasso had behaved in much the same way one day. She had followed him and found François lying in the path. Could it be happening again? She had never seen a person here although there had been signs. The washing on the line …

Eeyore took a few steps before standing firm, bobbing his shaggy mane and braying once more. His eyes never left her.

Kat put the apple back in her pocket and squeezed through the hedge. The paddock she found herself in was badly neglected and she stumbled from time to time over tussocks of weeds. When she reached Eeyore, he nuzzled her pocket for his treat before poking her along and trudging beside her to the tired-looking villa.

She hollered, then knocked on the door after receiving no response.

Eeyore nudged her again.

She slowly pushed open the door and stepped into a surprisingly pristine and welcoming entrance hall, with enormous oil paintings of flowers on the walls: hibiscus, poppy, sunflower, agapanthus, and rose—grand, single blooms in vivid colors. They made her feel as if she had walked into a giant's perennial garden.

"Bonjour! Helloooo!" Katherine called again.

"Entrez, s'il vous plait!" An unexpectedly strong, but slightly muffled, woman's voice rang out.

Kat jumped in surprise at another bray right behind her. Eeyore was waiting at the door, shuffling nervously in the gravel .

"Entrez! Venez! Aidez-moi, merci!"

The voice was coming from behind a closed door at the far end of a long hallway leading off the entrance hall. And so was the sound of someone singing. Kat was startled by it, as it just didn't fit the scene. Bob Dylan? Really?

As she walked quickly down the hallway, the singing stopped, and Kat heard the woman call "C'est qui?" She answered in French, asking if she was all right. Then she frowned when the woman responded, this time in English with a heavy French accent. Just once, Kat thought, I'd like to be answered in French.

"I'm fine, but I'm locked in this room. Do you see a key on the floor? It's big and should be easy to find."

Kat spotted the enormous brass key right away and quickly put it in the keyhole and turned it. Then she turned it again. "Turn it once more," the woman said. "It takes three turns to open this monster."

Kat did so, and the door swung open to reveal a sparsely furnished, whitewashed, room, with skylights and a row of windows running under the ceiling along one wall, too high up for anyone to see out of them. Under the skylights were two tall easels, a wooden table covered with tubes of paint, tubs of brushes, and neat piles of white cloths. On a chest next to the table sat a turntable and a stack of vinyl record albums. *The Freewheelin' Bob Dylan* was on the top.

On the far side of the terracotta tile floor was an oversized daybed filled with bright throw pillows, in the midst of which a petite, elderly woman dressed all in white sat in the lotus position, looking like a small, aged Buddha.

"Merci, ma chérie! I am extremely happy to see you, and don't worry. I am fine."

"Really? How long have you been locked in here?"

"Since yesterday afternoon, thanks to the mistral. I had the door and the skylights open, and this massive door normally does not budge. The key is always in it because the lock is so ancient it is loose. There is une petite vrillette, a little beetle, a permanent resident inside the door by the lock who leaves a delicate deposit of sawdust each day."

Kat bent down to look inside the lock. The key slipped easily out of place, but she could see no sign of anything.

The woman chuckled. "Oh, you will never catch sight of her. I call her Bernice. She's been with me forever—a constant companion who requires no care.

"I never lock the door from the inside, but I do sometimes from the outside, which is why the key is on that side. Yesterday the mistral slammed the door shut. I heard the lock click in the door as the key fell out, and knew I was in trouble."

"But you don't seem too worried."

"Mon Dieu! Where are my manners?" The woman winced as she slowly unfolded her legs, and Kat reached out to help steady her as she got to her feet. Her head barely reached Kat's shoulders. Her white hair, which was wound in an elegant knot, framed her softly wrinkled face. Her bright eyes, the color of the provençal sky, studied Kat intently.

She reached for a cane propped against the daybed. "I am Simone Garnier. And you?"

Kat introduced herself, explaining she had befriended Simone's donkey. "He alerted me to a possible problem."

"Victor Hugo is a clever baudet."

"I've been calling him Eeyore," Kat said. "Perhaps he responded because it rhymes with Victor. But, Madame Garnier, tell me why you weren't worried."

"Please, chérie, call me Simone. I have no time for formalities."

Katherine smiled an acknowledgement and shared she was often called Kat. "Simone. Do you not have a cellphone?"

"I do have one, mais, malheureusement, it was not here in my studio. I keep forgetting where I put it. But tomorrow is Friday when Monsieur Rousseau delivers my groceries. He would have released me."

Gesturing to a counter in the corner, she said, "I have a water dispenser and a bowl of dates and nuts, so I knew I would be fine. I even have a w.c."—she nodded toward a door in the back wall—"Just no window to climb out, as if I could."

Kat smiled, already liking this tiny woman, who radiated such good karma.

As vivacious as she was, the elderly woman's body language spoke of pain. Her every movement was slow and deliberate.

"Allons, ma chère. Let me make some tea for us." She motioned to Kat to follow her back down the long hallway.

The front door was still open, and the donkey was standing as Kat had left him, scuffing gravel impatiently. He nickered as Simone went to him and rubbed his nose.

"Ah, Victor Hugo, mon petit. Merci. Thank you for taking care of me. Je t'aime."

Off the entrance hall was a sterile-looking kitchen. Simone gestured to it and said, "Please. There is a bowl of apples on the counter. Would you get two of them?"

After Victor Hugo had been sufficiently rewarded and given one last scratch, they went into the kitchen.

Kat saw a kettle on the counter. "Please sit down and let me make the tea."

"Eh bien. Then you can tell me your story and I will tell you mine. Everyone has one. Non?"

Simone settled into a chair by a window that overlooked the property and pointed to a bowl filled with greens on the table beside her. "Those herbs from my garden make the most delicious tea. Just put them in the teapot and, when the water is ready, let it steep for a few minutes."

After she filled the kettle, Kat stood beside the wooden counter taking in the purity of her surroundings. Every room she had seen so far was devoid of color, apart from the paintings, the pillows in the studio and the tubes of paint. The whiteness of the walls was almost overpowering.

"I was not sure anyone lived here," Kat said, "but every now and then I noticed washing on the line."

"That's the way I like it. Very few people know. Most of the people I care about have left this earth, and I choose a life of seclusion with my art, my music and my memories."

"Aren't you lonely? Do you have any family?"

Simone pointed to a silver-framed photo on a shelf. "That is my son, Jean-Luc, and his partner, Olivier. We lived in adjoining apartments in the sixth arrondissement for decades and had such a fine time. He was the light of my life, and Olivier was like a son to me as well." A whistle pierced the air. "Ah, the kettle."

Kat filled the teapot and brought it to the table. She had noted Simone used the past tense.

Simone told her where to find cups, adding, "You will not want to add anything to this tisane, I assure you." Her eyes wrinkled with amusement but then changed as her voice became somber. "Jean-Luc and Olivier were killed in an auto accident."

"I'm so sorry. How tragic."

"It was twenty-four years ago. Some days it feels as if it was twenty-four hours ago. The ache can be sharp and immediate. Such is grief."

Kat sat down across the table from her, and their eyes met. She was feeling a stab of pain herself, her own grief summoned to the surface momentarily.

"I understand," she said.

"I can see you have felt the anguish of loss."

"Yes, but not the loss of a child. I can't imagine –"

"I am sorry. It is never easy."

Kat's eyes filled with tears, and she sniffed to hold them back.

Simone reached over and patted her hand. "Only those who have experienced grief understand. Take a minute. Perhaps we both need to."

They sat in silence for a moment, before Simone continued.

"I lived through the war," she said. "I learned the agony of loss, and how to survive it, during those years." Her eyes darkened.

Kat had seen that look before. Throughout her life. It would come and go in her parents' eyes. It was the scar of war. Memories that could never be erased.

"Those experiences helped me to go on when Jean-Luc was killed, although the pain was unique in its enormity. I lost part of myself as well.

"Hélas, he was my only child. My lifeline really. But he—and Olivier—left me with memories that keep me going. I left Paris for good after their accident and have lived here ever since. Every morning I wake up I know I must be here for a reason, and I welcome that. I have no room for bitterness."

Simone gazed at Kat, her eyes conveying her meaning more than any words could, then her face lit up with a smile. "Eh bien, now we must talk about happier things. Tell me about you."

Kat told her how her parents had also been survivors of the war, before giving her an abbreviated version of how she came to be in Antibes.

"Ah, so you are the lover of Philippe, the fabled fromager. I knew him as a child but he would not remember me."

"I must tell him. He has no idea anyone is living here."

"I have not wanted to be found. I am rather like his grandfather's property next door—left to languish for some time."

"Did you know his grandfather?"

"Oui, but that is a conversation for another time." She raised her hand to indicate the subject was closed. "I hear you are the talk of the village."

Kat cringed.

"And the terrible explosion," Simone said. "I was shocked. I understand Gilles was not hurt. Grâce à Dieu! It's not often something like that happens in our town. That is normally saved for Nice and Cannes, and then I hear it on the news on my radio or read it on the Internet."

"It was not as bad as it sounded," Kat said. "Something to do with the electrical wiring of a new alarm system."

"Although I seldom go out," Simone continued, "I hear much. Some things have not changed for centuries in la vieille ville. Gossip is one. J'adore les cancans! Philippe is much loved, and people are curious."

Kat blushed and she looked down at her hands. "Really? I'm embarrassed to think so many people are interested."

"Take it as a compliment, chérie. I, too, have been the subject of much gossip for most of my life. What fun it is to live a life that gives others the pleasure of conversation. Now pour us each a cup of this magic potion."

Kat closed her eyes at the taste. "Mmmm. Nectar of the gods."

"Une bonne bouche," Simone said.

Both women sipped in silence for a minute, and Kat looked around her at the small paintings on the kitchen walls. "These colors fill the room with such light and energy. They are truly joyful," she said.

"There is no pain in my work now," Simone said. "After the war, much of my work was very dark. For a few years after Jean-Luc died, I could not paint at all. When I began again, I decided to express only joy, and so now I summon only radiant reminders of the past. There were so many wonderful times."

They talked for a while about composition, color and inspiration, and the more Simone said, the more Kat felt drawn to her, impressed by her relaxed and positive outlook on life and on creating art.

Kat stood to leave after two refills of tea, not wanting to overstay her welcome.

"Thank you for listening to Victor and releasing me from my confinement," Simone said. "It was hardly a calamity, as I had what I needed. I often stay all day and night in my studio when I am painting. In fact, I was inspired to begin something new while I was shut in.

Between painting, meditating, and sleeping, I was a contented captive."

"Are you certain you will be fine? Is there someone I can call?"

"Chérie, I am as fine as I am on any other day. My needs are few and well taken care of. I enjoyed our visit. If you would like to share a cup or two of tea again another afternoon, please do come back."

"I would like that, thank you."

Simone wrote something down on a notepad and slid the page across the table. "Here's my cell number. Call me first, but do come again."

Kat wrote her number on another page. "And you must call me any time I can be of help."

Simone began to stand up, but Kat put out her hand. "Please don't get up. I will let myself out."

"Merci, chérie. À bientôt."

Simone explained there was a short path at the front of the house, which could not be seen from where Kat had found Eeyore.

The path led to a long driveway, ending at a locked gate, which Kat realized was on a different street than Philippe's property. The gate was slowly swinging open as she approached. Overgrown shrubs and grasses camouflaged where one had to turn in from the street and a sharp turn was necessary to get around them. She could see how it would easily be missed.

"It was quite remarkable," she told Philippe that evening at home, as he poured their apéros. "Simone Garnier must be getting on. I'm guessing she is at least in her mid-eighties, but she has a luminescent beauty about her that some women that age have. It shines from within and wraps itself around you in her presence. She is an intriguing woman, and her paintings burst with color and passion. I want to get to know her better."

"There you go again. Yet another adventure."

Kat took a long sip of her pastis. "My life here is definitely not dull," she said.

Philippe had been stunned to hear that someone lived on that property. And a little worried. "I wonder if she has ever noticed any activity in the cove by Dimitri's gang," he said. "I guess she wouldn't pay attention to it anyway if she is housebound. The house is far enough away from the water, and I believe the view is blocked by trees."

"Well, she doesn't miss much. She has her sources, from what she said. If she had seen anything, she probably would have alerted the police about it."

He shrugged. "They appear to be completely ignorant about anything going on down there, but now they are watching."

"Do we need to be worried?"

Philippe shrugged again, in the typical Gallic manner, with his arms spread and his hands open. "They assure me they have their best undercover team on the case, and we are not to be worried."

"Then let's not be," Kat said, still surprised she was not feeling more anxious about it.

"Her land adjoins ours along the length of the property line, but it is quite thickly forested until a point down by the water. There is a dilapidated boathouse and a stone storage barn down there, but nothing else. Until you discovered your donkey friend, there was never any sign of life. You will have to show me the driveway entrance tomorrow. It's such a surprise."

14

A few days later, Philippe was called to Nice to be questioned about Dimitri and Idelle, even though it had been years since he had seen either one. He also had to look through police photos to see if he could identify anyone connected to them.

"The narcs, as you call them, have been after this gang for a very long time," Philippe explained over dinner that night, "but they have been a slippery bunch. Dimitri is one of the kingpins of the drug trade now, and has built quite a fortress around him. This may be their first break in trapping him."

"And what are we to do while this operation is ongoing?"

"They've put some undercover security people at the market, and someone will be assigned to watch us."

"That's scary."

"I agree, but they said we would never know their people were around. There is one thing they have asked me to do. They want me to go to Lyon to speak with Denise to find out if she knows anything. I have to be casual about it. If she really knows nothing, they don't want her to learn about it from me. Do you want to come with me and help with the charade?"

"Lyon? Yes, please. Not exactly the circumstances I'd pick, but I'm in."

"I'll see when works best for Denise and Armand. You'll like them. I do. It's the older generation that's causing the problem."

They cleared the table and took their unfinished glasses of wine into the salon.

"Now I have a surprise," Philippe said. "Close your eyes. This will take a few minutes."

Kat could hear boxes being set down and a great deal of paper rustling, but despite her curiosity, she kept her eyes shut.

"Eh bien, mon amour. Regarde!"

A smile spread across her face as she saw he had set up a primitive papier maché crèche on the mantle. He'd placed several small clay figures around it, and she moved closer to examine them.

"Santons!" she exclaimed. "They are so sweet."

Philippe grinned. "Oui, santons. Small saints. My parents and I spent many messy days making this crèche, and they insisted that we use it year after year. For a while, as a teenager, it was an embarrassment for me. You know how that is."

"It's obviously been a treasure ever since," she said.

He told her how Adorée had refused to make a new one when she was a child. From the beginning, she too had wanted to use only this one, and it had been carefully stored away every year. Instead, with a little help, she had made some barns and stables, to add to the Christmas setting.

Ever since Philippe had told her the story of Viv and her final days, Kat was aware of a slight change in his demeanor around the topic. It seemed as if he'd relieved himself from the tremendous pressure he put himself under all those years when he kept the real story of his wife's illness a secret.

His excited voice broke into her thoughts, and she was soon caught up in his enthusiasm. "There are a lot more santons in the box. Tiens, help me put them out. I only did a few as a surprise. I thought we would set up the rest together."

Kat opened another bottle of wine. Philippe lit the fire. Soon the mantle was covered with the painted clay figures, none more than two inches high, representing village characters from the eighteen and nineteenth centuries: farmers, fishmongers, a doctor, a priest, a wine merchant, a teacher, a shepherd, a few children, musicians and dancers, along with an assortment of farm animals.

"At home, the crèches only have biblical figurines," Kat said, picking up a miller with a sack over his shoulder. "Their faces are all so expressive. The painting is simple but yet so detailed."

"En fait, the whole social structure of a Provençal village is here, all ages and occupations. During the Revolution, when churches were being looted and practicing religion was forbidden, people began to make crèches secretly in their homes. Later, as santons grew in popularity, some would even resemble celebrities. Families pass them from one generation to the next."

She inspected each one carefully.

"The painted figures are santons d'argile and the ones with fabric clothes are santons habillés," Philippe said.

"They are so detailed. J'adore tous."

Closer to Christmas, he explained, they'd place the holy family around the manger in the centre. Then, at midnight on Christmas Eve, they would add the baby Jesus, along with the three kings and an assortment of angels. "That's how we do it in our family, but everyone is different."

Kat laughed. "You're going to need to extend the mantle if you add any more to your collection."

"You'll find some irresistible ones when I take you to the Foire aux Santons in Marseille," he told her and grinned as she clapped her hands in delight at the news of another trip. "Then, if you like, we'll go on up to Aubagne. That's where we will find some of the finest santons. Some families there have been crafting them for generations, ever since the first ones were shown in Marseille in 1803."

Kat hugged Philippe, she was so excited.

They finished the wine while they decided when they would make this trip. Their calendar was quickly filling up. As the market was closed on Mondays, they decided that would be the day to go out of town.

Later that evening, the throwaway phone rang. They both stopped what they were doing and looked at each other. Philippe answered it and had a brief, terse conversation while he wrote something on a piece of paper. Kat was surprised that the call ended with him laughing.

"Tim and Twig send their love," he said. "They are well but longing for a fresh baguette from le Palais du Pain. They hope to be back by the summer. Tim says that Nick has information for us. I told him we are going to Marseille and he gave me a number to call when we get there. Someone will meet us."

"It's good news that they plan to be back here in the summer, but this is all sounding very cloak and daggerish," Kat said.

At 9:30 the following Monday, once rush hour had eased on the autoroute, they headed off on the two-hour drive to Marseille. Cold weather had set in, and they were bundled up.

"I've both read and heard that Marseille is not the safest place to visit. Some say that it's best avoided," Katherine said.

"Pffft!" Philippe shrugged. "Every city has its rough spots, and Marseille is no different. But not every city has the history and character of this grande dame. You will find it is a welcoming place"—he chuckled—"as long as you are not from Paris."

He glanced at her and saw her puzzled look. "The two cities have been archrivals forever. Parisians say Marseille is sleazy. Marseillais say Paris is snooty. The bottom line these days, à mon avis, is the rivalry between their football teams—that's soccer to you—Paris Saint-Germain and Olympique de Marseille. It's intense, very intense."

With a grin, Philippe nudged her, "Ne t'inquiète pas. Don't worry. With your accent, no one will think you are from Paris."

Kat snorted and punched him on the arm. "Too true!"

"You know, Marseille was the 2013 European City of Culture. That included the surrounding area over to La Ciotat and up to Aix."

"I read that in Nice-Matin. I get all the good info from my morning newspaper. You know, I think M. Bouchard is beginning to like me. He almost smiled the other day."

Philippe laughed. "M. Bouchard is an old softie under that tough exterior. He used to be my football coach back in the day, as you say."

It took them a while to wend their way into Marseille's old quarter and to find a parking spot. Eventually, in a way Kat could never quite understand, Philippe squeezed the car into what seemed like an impossibly small space.

"It's a French talent," he told her.

Even on a weekday morning, there was a festive atmosphere down la Canebière, the mile-long street that runs through the old part of town. It was lined with covered stalls where santonniers displayed their wares. The air was filled with laughter and the cheery calls of vendors.

Philippe called the number Tim had given him. They arranged a rendezvous with Nick's contact in an hour's time at a specific food stall. Tim gave him detailed instructions: "Order three pieces of pissaladière and sit at the back, at the last table by the garbage bins. Put one piece on a separate tray with an espresso."

"But who is meeting us?" Katherine asked him, after he told her. "It's not the most pleasant spot to sit. Maybe that's why they picked it."

"Aucune idée —I've no idea. We will just have to go there and see what happens."

"Now I'm hoping the undercover guys really are watching us."

They walked on, through a lively Christmas market at the far end of la Canebière, where excited children were lined up for rides on traditional roundabouts and were entertained by street musicians and clowns while they waited.

They were both jittery, so they stopped at a coffee bar but discovered they could not sit still. Quickly draining their cups, they strolled back and paused at a few stalls for distraction.

"I can't believe the variety of the santons," Katherine exclaimed, as they made their way along the street, but she resisted buying any and soon they arrived at the specified food stall.

Philippe ordered the three slices of pissaladière, the traditional snack he'd been told to buy, and they carried their trays to the patio behind the stall, where a few tables were being warmed by a heater, and sat down at the table Tim had mentioned.

"If anyone ever told me I would enjoy eating anchovies and onions for breakfast, I would have thought they were crazy. And even more crazy if they'd added that I would be meeting a mysterious stranger, possibly a criminal, in Marseille, while eating it next to garbage bins." Kat laughed nervously, and Philippe put his arm around her.

The patio was jammed with people, and two others joined their table, leaving a few empty seats between them. Philippe put the separate tray next to his place.

After a few minutes, a man in a long dark coat, scarf, woolen hat and sunglasses slid into the chair next to Philippe. His hat was pulled down almost to his glasses, hiding most of his face. Stubble, too long to be fashionable, covered his cheeks and chin.

He pulled the tray roughly toward him and said, "Merci. J'ai faim."

Then he looked at Kat. "As gorgeous as ever."

Kat gasped, "Nick! Oh my god, it's you," before she put her hand over her mouth and looked to see if anyone was listening.

Philippe attempted to stifle his surprise. "Incroyable!" he whispered, his eyes about to pop. "You're the last person we expected. Are you okay? Is it safe for you to be here?"

"Ah, mes amis, Marseille takes care of me. You know how it is here. Money talks. I'm okay, mate. I flew in only to see you two and give you this."

He picked up a napkin and, with a sleight of hand, tucked a piece of paper into it before sliding it under Philippe's tray. "When you get up, pick that napkin up with the others and slip it in your pocket when you throw the rest in the garbage. You can do it."

He grinned at them. "It's so good to see you both, and I'm happy to hear you are together. Sorry about this mess you're in, and I hope I can help. I've given you the private cellphone number for Inspecteur Roget Thibideau, who is a reliable senior member of the narcotics division in Paris. He is smart and honest—that's the key. And he would love to get this gang. He will contact you directly, but if you don't hear from him within three days, call him at that number."

Philippe began to thank Nick, but he was already on his feet, gulping his espresso as he got ready to leave.

"Gotta get out of here. I've got my chartered plane waiting. I'm going straight to Oz. I'll be back in Antibes in the summer."

Kat had been sitting speechless. Stunned, really. Finally she spoke to Nick, "We're so happy to see you and to know things are okay with you. What a reunion we will have next summer. Thanks for helping."

Nick spoke into a napkin as he wiped his lips with it. "No worries but be careful. These people can be dangerous. Do exactly what Thibideau says."

With that he turned his back, tossed his napkin and paper plate into the bin and disappeared into the crowd.

Kat and Philippe stared at each other in astonishment.

"This just keeps getting crazier."

"God bless Nick. What a good guy."

They agreed that they might as well carry on with their day, and as they stood to leave Philippe slipped the napkin from under the tray and into his pocket. Then he tossed the others, along with the uneaten pissaladière, into the bin. They had completely forgotten the food during the rendezvous.

Their plan was for Kat to choose two santons at this market, and then they would drive the short distance to the historic hillside village of Aubagne to check out its pottery shops.

Kat was overwhelmed at the selection in the stalls along la Canebière. The enormous variety of sizes, paint styles, and characters made choosing just two a challenge.

"I'm sorry but I need to look at them all to make sure I am not missing anything."

"Choose as many as you want, then, Minou."

Every once in a while they would look at each other, raise their eyebrows and shake their heads. One or the other would say,

"Incroyable" or "I don't believe it." But she did finally pick four, and soon they were on their way to Aubagne, a short drive from the city.

"Promise me we'll have time to visit the house where Marcel Pagnol was born," Kat asked as they drove through the countryside immortalized in his beloved stories Jean de Florette and Manon des Sources.

They visited a number of ceramics studios, where they admired the craftsmanship and bought a few more irresistible santons, then managed to tear themselves away in time for a quick visit to Pagnol's birthplace. Several rooms in the townhouse where the writer was born had been furnished with original pieces.

"I'm so glad we had time for that," Kat said afterward. "The video presentation was a nice touch."

Philippe agreed. "And dinner will be even better. J'ai faim!"

He was true to his word, although they could not stop talking about Nick through the entire meal at a small bistro in the picturesque Place Joseph Rau.

As they drove home, Kat examined their ten new santons, before her thoughts turned again to their unexpected meeting with Nick.

"This is unreal," she said. "And I'm not talking about the santons."

"Well, I am. I think we lost control," Philippe laughed. "I might have to extend the mantle, after all. But just in case we need more, the Foire aux Santons in Aix opens in two weeks."

They looked at each other and grinned. "I can't believe we are being so relaxed about this right now. It's bizarre."

"We have our moments," Philippe said. "I'm anxious to talk to this Inspecteur Thibideau. Maybe then we will begin to get somewhere."

"I hope so. Now about these santons, let's set them up as soon as we get home, chez nous." Kat yawned and snuggled into her seat for a nap. Philippe reached over to pull her closer, gently tousling her hair.

"Chez nous," he repeated softly. "Home. We are going to have a very joyeux Noël, I promise you that."

"That's a promise to keep," Katherine whispered.

15

Calendales, the period of Christmas celebration, began in earnest on December 4, the feast day of la Sainte Barbe. In every home and shop window, on the counter at la Poste, on the bar at every one of the cafés Kat frequented and even in the windows of the patisseries, saucers of sprouting lentils and wheat seeds were on display. Everywhere she looked, a mini wheat field was sprouting.

Joy had explained on the phone. "It's a tradition that goes back to Roman times. The sprouts are carefully nurtured, and if they grow straight and green, there will be a bountiful harvest in the coming year. If they go yellow or droop over, then that's bad news. Some of the wheat is used to decorate tables and crèches on Christmas Eve, but most bunches are wrapped with a red ribbon and cared for right through to la Chandeleur, la Fête de la Lumière, on February 2."

Philippe insisted there was one more aspect to growing the Sainte Barbe wheat that she needed to know. "Every day you must hold the wheat between you and your lover and kiss passionately. This makes the wheat grow strong and healthy."

Kat never refused.

On the morning of December 4, she phoned Simone to invite herself for tea that afternoon. She had been thinking about her a great deal, and she and Philippe had been by the gate a few times during the week, so she had no difficulty finding it now.

Since the mistral, the weather had remained chilly, and Kat was bundled up. It felt more like fall in Canada than the weather she associated with the Côte d'Azur, a feeling accentuated by the faint smell of a wood fire.

Simone had described how to find a hidden call button. Kat pressed it now and the gate slowly opened. As she walked down the driveway, Kat noticed a lane leading off it, away from the house, and made a mental note to tell Philippe that it appeared to be used. She also noticed fresh tire tracks on the driveway and thought perhaps the grocer had visited Simone.

Simone was beaming as she reached up, from a wheelchair, to bise Katherine at the door. "Chérie, I hoped I would hear from you again soon," she said, tilting her head.

"Et voilà! Here I am!"

Kat handed her a small package that contained everything for Simone to start her own saucer of Sainte Barbe wheat.

"Thank you. Shall I open it now? Please excuse my wheels. Some days when my arthritis is bad, I find this makes it easier to move around."

"And why not? I think it's a very wise idea."

At the table, Simone unwrapped the gift while Kat plugged in the kettle. "How thoughtful. What memories this brings back. It's been a long time since I celebrated la Sainte Barbe."

While the tea steeped, Kat talked about her visit to the Foire aux Santons and how much she was loving the holiday traditions in France. Simone listened, with the same wistful expression on her face that Kat had seen during her first visit.

"Do you have a collection of santons?" she asked

"Hélas, my crèche and santons have not seen the light of day since Jean-Luc died."

She looked past Katherine and began to speak in a soft voice. "For two years after the war, I remained in Normandy. There was much work to be done. Much healing—for the people, for the country, for our hearts ..." Her voice drifted off and she sat quietly in thought.

Kat waited for her to speak again.

"Many of us had spent years together in the Resistance. Some could not wait to leave when the battle was over, but others of us could not bear to leave. I had a lover, and we remained together until we were strong enough to go our separate ways. He had a life to return to, and I was not part of it."

Simone's words were passionate but tempered with wisdom.

"I finally returned to Paris in 1949 and moved in with my mother. I was twenty-nine. My mother was alone after my father had died of a heart attack during the Occupation. They had a rambling apartment in the Sixth, which had been in her family since the Revolution. Later, after Jean-Luc was an adult, we made it into two—but I digress. Those post-war years were a magical time to live in Paris, and the Sixth was alive with the arts. Writers, artists and thinkers, the intellectuals of the day, endlessly debated the philosophies of the time. Le Café de Flore and les Deux Magots were just down the street from us and they were constantly abuzz—electric, really."

As Simone spoke of the excitement of those heady years in Paris, Kat was reminded of that sense of a new dawn in her own life.

"I read so much about those post-war years," she said, "and studied them at university. I wrote many papers on Jean Paul Sartre and his revival of existentialist thinking. I found his writing intellectually intoxicating, and yet I married someone who didn't get it and frowned upon the entire movement. I know now I should never have been with him. But I had led a relatively sheltered childhood and chose to study when others my age were partying."

Speaking in generalities at first, Kat was soon baring her soul. She felt a trusting intimacy with Simone, and found herself expressing thoughts she had never voiced before.

The teapot was replenished.

"I feel now that I have control of my life. I'm open to change and to opportunities, and it is so liberating."

"Don't lose it now that you have found it."

Kat could see Simone was starting to get tired.

"I should be going. Please tell me if there is anything I can do for you."

"You are right, chérie. I do lie down in the afternoon. It's another of the joys of aging."

During their chat, Kat had worked out that Simone was ninety-four, and she was stunned. Now another thought came to her. "The next time I come, would you like me to help you set up your crèche?"

Simone paused and then nodded. "Come again when you can, Katherine. I had forgotten how pleasurable it is to chat with another woman you like. Eh bien, I will tell you the next chapter."

Kat had hoped Simone would continue her story, but did not want to ask in case it appeared rude. She was captivated by this woman and the stories she had told so far, and couldn't wait to hear what happened next.

But she had another reason to come back. She was feeling concerned about her new friend now that she was aware that drug smuggling was going on so close to her house.

16

The following day, Philippe said, "Pack for two days, Minou. You will need warm clothes and good walking shoes. The day after tomorrow we will go to Lyon. We'll take the train.

"I knew it was on your list of places you wish to visit," he grinned. She threw her arms around him and whispered "wish list."

"This isn't exactly the best reason to take a trip, but we'll manage," she said after Philippe explained the plan. He had told his cousins they were coming so that they could meet Kat and show her their beautiful city.

"We will be enthusiastic tourists for two days," he said. "During that time I have to attempt to get as much information—casually—from Denise about Idelle's whereabouts. Apparently, she and Dimitri moved from Normandy two years ago and the police have not been able to trace them. They suspect they are running things from Russia."

"I can play along, no problem. Still can't believe all this, though."

Kat settled into her comfortable seat on the TGV, glad to be back on the train for the first time since her trip from Avignon to Paris at the end of her first exchange. Philippe had booked first-class seats on the upper deck so they could have the best view.

After an unimpressive departure between blocks of fairly modern apartments in the upper part of Antibes, the train hugged the narrow sandy beaches that lined the coast from Juan-les-Pins west to Cannes. The early morning rays reflecting off the sea made them squint as they took in the lovely coastal views.

"I'm surprised that people still come to sit on the beach at this time of year. Some of them are even swimming. And the fishermen just bundle up and keep setting their lines, " Kat said.

Philippe laughed. "Bien sûr! Fishing never stops. Some of the locals are diehards and take a dip no matter what. The Germans and Scandinavians don't seem to care how cold it is."

Not long after the stop in Cannes, the scenery changed dramatically as they passed through rock cuts and tunnels in le massif de l'Esterel. Kat noticed that the morning sun was coaxing a startling range of shades from the distinctive red, craggy hills.

At times, the train wound out of the hills to present them with spectacular views of sparkling coves, some filled with moored boats and others solitary and inviting. Here the Med was a deep azure where the water met the jagged shoreline.

"The change from the turquoise of Antibes and Nice is so dramatic," Kat exclaimed. "It's a very different kind of beauty."

Philippe nodded. "There are many who prefer one area to the other. Often with great vehemence."

A brief stop in Saint Raphael signaled a change of scene, as the train moved away from the sea for a while until it neared Toulon. They sped past quiet hamlets and farms with low outbuildings, surrounded by seemingly endless rows of grapevines, some still showing their autumn colors. They passed olive groves and fields green with winter wheat, and spotted, here and there, the last of the season's figs still stubbornly clinging to branches.

Kat was enchanted to see several villages perched on outcroppings or huddled in wide valleys and was reminded of the strict regulations in France that control the colors of walls, shutters and roofs. There were isolated, vine-covered, stone farmhouses and rambling barns that led her to wonder about the histories forever captured in their thick walls. A glimpse of the particular blue of a swimming pool at times made it clear the ancient and the new co-existed, if not always happily.

"As they should," Philippe said when Kat remarked on the contrast. "Ancient plumbing is not romantic, in spite of how you see it."

Rocky outcroppings came into view occasionally and forested hills appeared as they neared Toulon and moved well into the Var region. Philippe pointed to some good hiking areas they might try one day.

He explained that their timing for this trip to Lyon was perfect, as they would be there during the renowned Fête des Lumières, when much of the city and many of its most beautiful buildings were lit with spectacular displays of colorful lights, many of them animated and set to music. "It's going to be crowded. People come from all around the world to see the lights. Millions of them. The fête lasts four days and there's a massive party throughout the city. You have to make restaurant reservations months in advance—unless you know my cousin Armand.

"The legend is that the Virgin Mary saved the city from the plague and, to thank her, a statue was built in 1852. On the day it was erected, the whole city was lit by candles that its citizens had put in their windows."

After leaving Marseille, the train turned north, its engine kicked into high gear and le Train à Grande Vitesse lived up to its name.

Philippe dug into his backpack and pulled out a gift-wrapped package. "You'll like this."

"Forgive me if I don't talk much for the rest of the trip," Kat said, after she had unwrapped a guidebook to Lyon, and she spent much of the rest of the journey reading about the history of the city.

The first time she looked up was when the train stopped in Aix-en-Provence. Katherine was surprised by how soon they had reached the town.

"Only ten minutes! But I didn't see Sainte-Victoire," she said. "We always see it on the drive."

The barren, imposing Montagne Sainte-Victoire near Aix, painted more than two hundred times by Cezanne, commanded their attention whenever they went there by car but was nowhere to be seen from the train.

"Instead I'm looking at a nuclear reactor. It's not the same," she said and buried herself back in the book. From time to time, Philippe nudged her to enjoy the scenery.

Fields of dried sunflowers reminded Kat of the golden vistas of Provence in June. Most of the fields were brown or yellow and looked dry, including vast vineyards at rest for the winter.

"Fields of solar panels aren't on my wish list of things to see," she muttered as they passed a huge installation.

"But they are part of modern life," Philippe said. "Just like those windmills over there, providing electricity with today's technology."

"Noooo," Katherine cried. "I only want to see the Don Quixote type of windmills, merci beaucoup."

Philippe shook his head. "Une vraie romantique."

The hills of the Luberon, still green in spite of winter's approach, appeared in the distance as the train approached Valence. Soon they were traveling through a vast patchwork of fields that were mute testimony to the agricultural importance of the area. Tractors and other heavy machinery were at work, turning the fields and preparing furrows for spring planting. Katherine set the book aside and, undeterred by the windows, took several photos.

"The shutter in my eye never stops when I'm in a landscape like this," she said. "Let's come back in the spring by car, so we can stop at these old farms and explore the roads."

"Avec plaisir."

When the view again became unremarkable, Kat continued reading.

Some minutes later, she rested the open book in her lap. "I just read that Lyon was the heart of the Resistance during the Second World War. That movement fascinates me. One of the first places I want to visit is the Resistance Museum."

"I'm putting it on the list."

Suddenly the countryside vanished, and the train slowed down as it passed through the industrial areas on the outskirts of Lyon. Finally, the train stopped, and they stepped into one of the biggest and most crowded stations she had ever seen.

Philippe hailed a taxi outside the vast station for the final leg of their journey to Denise and Armand's apartment on the edge of the old town. Soon they were climbing the four flights of stairs to their front door.

"This is another good reason to pack lightly when traveling in France." Kat said, stopping to catch her breath, even though Philippe was carrying her bag. "And I thought I was in good shape!"

"Stair climbing requires a special breathing technique," Philippe teased.

The apartment door was ajar and, when she heard them arrive, Denise dashed out to greet them, while Armand held the door open wide.

"Pas juste!" Denise exclaimed when Philippe told her they would only be staying for two days. "We want more time to get to know cette charmante femme, who has captured your heart. You must promise to come again, and soon."

"We will," Philippe said. "We can't possibly see everything in this short a time."

Denise was as exuberant as her pixie-like appearance suggested. She was petite, with closely cropped dark hair that was streaked with pink and plum. Her violet eyes sparkled as she spoke, while her hands motioned non-stop.

Armand was short and sturdily built, with a quiet expression that belied a sense of humor as robust as his appetite. His closely-shaven head and wire-rimmed glasses enhanced his academic appearance. He had studied in California and his English was excellent.

After Philippe and Kat put their bags in the office-cum-guest room and freshened up, the foursome headed out.

"Katherine, next year you and Philippe must come in November for le Beaujol'ympiades. It's when we celebrate the arrival of the year's

Beaujolais Nouveau. The parties are très amusantes," Denise said. They were walking through the old town and had stopped to look at one of the many posters announcing the previous month's festivities.

Armand nodded, "No one welcomes le Beaujolais Nouveau better than the Lyonnais."

Katherine smiled at this display of the love the French have for their wines, and the warmth of the cousins' welcome allayed the slight anxiety she'd been feeling at the prospect of meeting Philippe's wife's family.

First on their hosts' agenda as tour guide was a bus tour, to give them a sense of the city's layout and an opportunity to see some of its enormous trompe l'oeil wall murals.

"We have a history of wall painting here, dating back to the Romans," Armand said. "There are over two hundred outdoor murals, and some of our modern fresco painters are known throughout the world. Did you know we are a UNESCO World Heritage Site?"

He was obviously proud of his city. And he had good reason to be, Kat thought. It was a lovely place, and the nineteenth-century architecture at its heart reminded her a little of Paris. "The main difference that I can see," she said, "is all the avant-garde installations."

"There's some cutting-edge art here, bien sûr," Denise said. "A good example is what's happening in the new area of Confluence in the Presqu'île district, where the Rhône and the Saône rivers join together. There used to be only slaughterhouses and prisons there, but it's being redeveloped and promises to be a showcase of modern architecture. There's an eclectic mix of style in Lyon."

Armand pointed out the imposing Basilica of Notre-Dame de Fourvière, which overlooked the city from atop a hill in the old quarter.

"It makes me think of Sacré Coeur, except it is all towers instead of domes," Kat said.

"We lovingly refer to it as l'éléphant renversé, the upside-down elephant!"

"Some of us do," corrected Denise, poking him in the ribs. "Personally, I love its look."

The bus drove on through narrow streets lined with five-story buildings to la place des Terreaux. The openness of the square tempted them off the bus for an espresso break in a café near the impressive fountain of a woman driving four charging horses.

"Here's what you should know about this square," Armand said once they were settled inside the café. "It was originally the site of the pig market, because you know Lyon is famous for its pork, and also of public executions. The two weren't held on the same day, I don't think. We don't hold either of them any more, for which the pigs thank us, I'm sure."

He grinned, and Denise snorted, "Ask me how many times I've heard these stories."

"So, to continue, the intricate sculpture in the fountain is the work of Bartholdi, creator of the Statue of Liberty, and it represents the Garonne river and its four tributaries rushing to the sea. But you must see it lit up at night."

"He's right," Denise agreed. "C'est incroyable."

"Merci à mon assistante," Armand said, raising his cup in a toast. Denise stood and curtsied.

Armand cleared his voice and went on. "The Hôtel de Ville, that exquisite edifice you see at the end of the square, which is our city hall, was first constructed in the mid 1600s. Twenty-five years later, a fire destroyed most of it, but it was rebuilt shortly afterward. In 1792, during the sitting of the Revolutionary Court, our national anthem, the Marseillaise, was sung in public here for the first time. Lots of towns, and Paris of course, like to claim to be the first … and so do we!"

He proceeded to sing a few bars and Philippe joined in to give Kat a rousing rendition, while Denise buried her face in her hands. Their laughter prompted people at several other tables to join in.

Fully re-caffeinated, they waited at the bus stop to continue the tour.

As they left the square, Denise said, "He didn't mention that the carillon in l'Hôtel is one of the largest in Europe, with sixty-five bells.

It plays on Sunday evenings in the summer and once a week the rest of the year. It will play during the fête so you will hear it."

They left the bus tour again to explore the Renaissance district on foot. One of the oldest areas in Lyon, it was lucky enough to have survived for five hundred years almost intact. Armand explained that some of the buildings were erected in the Middle Ages and many more in the Renaissance era, when silk weaving and printing were the city's main industries.

"I love how they have made so many streets here only for pedestrians. Everything seems so accessible," Kat said. Then she remembered from what she's read that, hidden from view, were hundreds of secret, covered passageways, called traboules, that ran through private homes and down to the river, some of them dating back to the fourth century.

She had been unaware of Lyon's silk-weaving past until Véronique had talked about it in Entrevaux. The guidebook Philippe had given her on the train had several pages about that history, and she was particularly interested in seeing the traboules. She'd read that they had been used by the Resistance during the German occupation. She mentioned her interest to Armand, who told her that many of them were in the Croix-Rousse area, where they were headed next.

Walking through to Place Bellecoeur, the largest square, they went down into the subway and caught the next train. The district, built on a hill, was once the centre of the silk weaving industry. There was no time left to explore any of the traboules that were open to the public, so Denise suggested that Philippe take Kat on a tour of them the next day. "They are architecturally unique as well as historically important. You can't imagine what they are like until you see them for yourself."

While the men stopped into a bar, the women went on a guided tour of the Maison des Canuts, the Silk Weavers' House, where they looked at the many antique looms on display and watched a demonstration of how an old, treadle-operated dobby loom worked. "It's like watching an intricate ballet," she whispered to Denise. "The movements required are so precise and demanding. It's quite the workout for the weaver. The Jacquard looms are fascinating too, with those punch cards."

"Jacquard really was responsible for the whole idea of programming machines and his concepts were critical in the development of computing hardware," Denise said, as the tour finished, her enthusiasm matching Kat's. "I never tire of visiting this area. There's always something to learn."

The weather difference from the coast was a bit of a shock and reminded Kat of Toronto in December. She was glad Philippe had encouraged her to put a heavy sweater on under her jacket.

"My feet are ready for a rest," Denise exclaimed after they rejoined Philippe and Armand. "We've covered a lot of territory today."

They hailed a taxi and went back to the apartment to shower, change, warm up and enjoy an apéro."I'm sure you know the drill by now," Armand teased Kat, as he served them all a celebratory Kir Royale.

"Bien sûr," she replied. "Santé!"

This part of the day was another French tradition to which Kat had adapted, that was a complete change from the rush from work to dinner that was the rule in her marriage. James had not been a fan of cocktail hour.

Of course, that would have meant he had to converse with me, she thought ruefully.

Joy had explained the philosophy of l'apéritif in France to Katherine when she was first in Provence on her exchange.

"L'heure de l'apéro is not just a time for cocktails," she had said. "It is the moment when the French deliberately create some space between the workday and the dinner hour, demonstrating their talent for slowing down and, somehow, miraculously expanding time. The idea is to whet the appetite for the meal that is to come. Le plaisir … remember?"

Denise and Armand, expanded on the tradition.

They all raised their glasses, without actually making contact.

"Did you know that it is bad luck to cross arms with others when we reach across to toast," Denise said.

"Yes, I heard that," Kat said. "I also know we must always make eye contact with the person. It's one of the many lessons I've learned from Philippe."

"Ah, she is learning quickly to become française, Philippe."

"D'accord," he replied, his eyes shining.

The conversation turned to where to eat dinner that night, and Armand spoke persuasively in favor of their local bouchon, a kind of restaurant that served traditional Lyonnais food.

Denise held up a hand to get a word in. "Katherine, you should know that Armand is a bit like royalty here in Lyon, as he is descended from one of the original mères Lyonnaises, the local women employed as cooks by aristocratic families."

"I just read about them on the train."

"So you know that, after the Revolution, they were encouraged to write down their recipes—"

Armand broke in excitedly. "And my great-great-grandmother was one of those mères. Her recipes were handed down through my family but, of more pride to us, some of the greatest chefs in this city were trained following her strict rules."

"Armand's family is well-known here and is always welcome at the finest restaurants, sans réservations." Philippe added.

"So now you know why he is the way he is."

"You mean trop gros?" asked Armand, feigning hurt.

"Non, not overweight," Denise laughed, giving him a light poke in his well-padded stomach, "I mean why you are so fixated on cuisine."

Armand played along and doubled over before continuing, "Bien! So tonight, Katherine my dear, you will eat the food of the fine mères de Lyon. You will love it!"

"Tomorrow we will take you for a meal at the other end of the spectrum here. We will cover it all," Philippe promised, as his cousins nodded in agreement.

"C'est une visite éclair!" laughed Denise.

"A lightning visit," translated Armand.

"Right—a whirlwind visit," Kat offered.

They left for dinner at eight and strolled a few blocks to a small corner restaurant, where Armand pointed out the sticker on the window, indicating it was an authentic bouchon. They entered a packed, wood-paneled room, with tables covered in red-and-white checked cloths.

While they waited for the food to arrive, Philippe and Denise chatted while Armand told Kat the history of some of the more famous bouchons, many of which originally were small post houses or inns. A straw bottle stopper or bouchon would be hung in the window to indicate that meals were served.

"In the early days, these places served diners from every walk of life, some of them very unsavory. The secret was the food, prepared by a mère while the husband poured wine and collected the money. It's like sitting down for a family meal, but you have to pay for it.

"Each bouchon has its own ambiance, flavor and history," he added. "But there are two things they have in common—delicious traditional dishes and noise."

After a meal that included duck paté, sausages, roast pork and quenelles, they strolled along narrow laneways that were lit up for the fête. Philippe deliberately dropped behind his cousins and whispered to Kat that she was doing a fine job of distracting Armand.

"We've exchanged some nice memories about the family, but I'm not saying a word to Denise about Idelle until later tomorrow. I have always liked her and feel a bit of a heel to be doing this. But whatever will help, we must do. Thanks, Minou. You are making this all so much easier."

"Tonight we'll wander a few streets and tomorrow we will visit Notre-Dame, which is why we didn't get off the bus there earlier," Armand called back to them, pointing high above the rooftops at the basilica, glowing against the night sky. "There's been a shrine there since the eleventh century. Originally it was the site of the Roman forum; the basilica was built on top of an older structure to give thanks to the Holy Mary for the city being spared during the Franco-Prussian war of 1870, give or take a few years."

"Armand, you are the best tour guide. I can't believe how much we are squeezing in. The church looks spectacular," Kat said. "The view from up there must be incredible."

"On a clear day, you can see all the way to Mont Blanc."

"We'll take the funicular up the steep hill tomorrow. It will deposit us right at the front door," Denise said.

"Tomorrow is the eighth and that's the highlight of the fête. We'll see a spectacular son et lumières at la place des Terreaux. Je te promets." Philippe raised Kat's hand to his lips.

"But now it's time for un peu de jazz, old-time American style, don't you agree?" Armand said. He guided them into a dimly-lit, dark-paneled bar, where they caught the final set of a swing band before taking a taxi home.

At 8:00 the next morning, they left to explore the storied covered market, les Halles de Lyon, dedicated to the city's favored son, chef Paul Bocuse.

"Caffeine first," Armand said, "and then we will sample our way through the stalls. It's what we do." He led the way, waving his arm in the air while Denise rolled her eyes. Philippe took Kat's hand, as they followed along. "This is definitely his territory," he said.

Aisle after aisle was lined with stalls bursting with every culinary goodness imaginable.

"What shall we find for you, Minou? Macaron? Chocolat? Nougat? Oui? All of them?"

For himself, Philippe had one thing in mind: Fromagerie de La Mère Richard.

Armand's face glowed. "Ahhh, le Saint-Marcellin!"

Kat looked quizzically at Philippe, who explained, "Madame Renée Richard supplies cheese to all the top chefs in France. Her Saint-

Marcellin cheese is world famous and without compare. I have ordered from her but I've never met her in person. I hope she's here."

Armand charged ahead to the shop to tell Madame Renée who Philippe was, and as soon as the others arrived, she greeted Philippe and said how pleased she was to meet him. She cut him a generous sample of the cheese, then turned her attention to the long line of people awaiting her attention. Philippe understood completely.

He explained to Kat as he offered her a taste, "It's a small disk with a runny, strong, nutty center and a moldy rind that is cut off. See how it sticks to the knife? The texture is unique. The secret is in the ripening."

Her grin said everything as she slowly savored the taste.

Armand waved them along again. "Mission accomplished! On to the next gustatory delight."

All the food around them soon stirred their appetites and they stopped into the AOC restaurant, where Armand just happened to know the chef, for an early lunch. They were seated within minutes and served wine from thick-bottomed bottles called "pots." All of the food served there was provided by the market sellers, Armand explained. "Simplicity with quality," he said, as he made his suggestions. "My only rule is to save room for la tarte tatin, which is merveilleuse."

As they were running tight for time, they did not linger over their meals and soon they were in a taxi on their way to the funicular to take them up to the Notre-Dame basilica.

"It's a must," Denise said, "even if we have to rush a bit."

After a quick tour of the landmark church, which Kat thought was definitely not long enough, the two couples parted company. Denise had to go to work and Armand said that he had things to attend to. Kat and Philippe went on a tour of a few of the traboules.

Kat learned that the first traboules were built in the fourth century by area residents, who needed quick access to the Saône River for their water supply. These passageways were expanded upon later during the centuries of the silk trade. They allowed goods to be protected from the weather as they were moved between the canuts—the silk workers in the textile mills on the hill—and the merchants down by the river.

Their tour took them down one traboule that had been fully restored. They walked along stretches of narrow corridors that opened into courtyards or led to steps—in one case, to a spiral staircase—that took them down toward the river. At one point, Kat was delighted to find herself in an Italianate galley.

The tour guide told them stories that sounded like fiction to Kat. He described how, during the French Revolution, residents used the complex maze of passageways to hide from the enemy. Many people credited them for preventing the occupying Germans from taking complete control of this area of the city during the Second World War.

The tour ended near the river and from there they walked over to the Resistance museum. It was, as Kat expected, an emotional experience for her to see the exhibits about this dark time in history. By the time they returned to the apartment, they were exhausted in every way.

"Armand, please forgive us, but we cannot face going out for a fancy dinner this evening," Philippe said. "We need just to relax for a while before the lumières."

"That's a relief to hear," Armand said. "Denise called to say she has to stay a bit later at work, so we were thinking the same thing, but felt guilty about denying you a meal at a Michelin-starred restaurant while you are here. We will just have something light chez nous before we go out."

Later on, after Denise arrived, Kat discovered that the "something light chez nous" was a classic Lyonnais meal made with the food Armand had purchased at the market that morning. While they had been exploring the traboules, he had been cooking.

The first course was a foie gras mousse topped with aspic and apples. Then a slightly warmed Saint-Marcellin, lightly brushed with white wine, was served with toasted Poilâne, on greens that included chicory and arugula dressed with walnut oil, a squeeze of lemon, and toasted hazelnuts. A charcuterie plate accompanied the salad.

After dinner, they went out, and until well into the wee hours of the morning, they strolled from one imaginative son et lumières spectacle to another. A lot of the time, Katherine walked beside Armand to hear his detailed and entertaining explanations of everything. This gave Philippe the opportunity to talk more with Denise.

On their way back to the apartment, Kat became aware that the conversation between Philippe and Denise had taken a turn for the worse. She could not hear what was being said, as they were too far ahead, but she could tell from their body language and gestures that things had become tense.

Back at the apartment, Kat had the impression Denise had been crying. Goodnights were quickly exchanged in the dimly lit hall, leaving her no time to ask if all was well. Armand was leaving for a flight very early the next morning, and his invitation to them to return was warm and sincere.

Once they were alone, Philippe confirmed Denise had become quite irritated when he pressed her about Idelle. "I'm sure her mother knows where Idelle is. They're sisters, after all. Denise as much as said they have seen her. She obviously has been told Idelle's life is not up for discussion, but I honestly don't think she knows why."

He slipped into bed and wrapped his arms around her. "I guess I did upset her a bit, but even so she said they hope we will come for another visit, as long as next time I don't ask so many questions she can't answer. I felt badly."

The next morning, Denise seemed fidgety around Philippe. Kat sensed a definite reserve when she said goodbye, although she seemed sincere in her wishes for them to return.

Philippe was distracted on the return trip.

"Is something bothering you?" Kat asked. "I mean apart from the whole mess we have around us at the moment?"

"Rien du tout, Kat. It's nothing. I believe it's under control," he said.

She could tell from his frown and the set of his jaw, it was not nothing. It was definitely something.

Philippe took her hand and patted it, but it didn't erase her concern. "I was just thinking about work and the demands of the season," he said. "In fact, I had better spend this time on the train catching up."

He opened his computer and was soon absorbed in work.

Kat settled more deeply into her seat and watched the landscape flash by, although she really wasn't seeing it.

After Marseille, Philippe shut his laptop and put his arm around her shoulders, drawing her close and pressing his lips to her head.

"You are lost in thought, Minou. À quoi tu penses?"

Kat could not get out the words she wanted to say. "I'm just tired. It was a very busy two days. I hope the information you have will help the police investigation."

"Try not to think about it for now. We did what we could. Put your head on my shoulder and sleep. We've still got a couple of hours to go."

Kat pulled back and looked squarely at him. "Are we going to be able to make this threat go away? Do you believe the police will get to the bottom of it? I swing between being quite blasé about it and then feeling frightened. I'm still just not sure about what."

Philippe's face clouded. "I'm sorry I don't know the answer. Désolé. You were right earlier. This whole situation is bothering me a great deal. Perhaps you should go back to Toronto until it is resolved. I feel terrible about bringing this into your life."

Kat surprised herself with the ferocity of her reply. "I'm not leaving. We will work through this together. The police seem to have things under control, and we are being watched since the fire, so we are probably safe. I understand how you feel but it's not your fault really. Stuff happens. Just not usually quite this dramatically. Christmas is coming—our first together. I'm not going away."

17

As Christmas came closer, the atmosphere of the market in Antibes grew merrier. The lively good humor of both sellers and their customers seemed to reach new heights. Kat pitched in to help make the look festive, unpacking barrels filled with decorations. Soon twinkling lights, bright tinsel garlands, and decorative combinations of fruits, vegetables and evergreen boughs festooned the stalls and walkways. The vast space was transformed.

Laughter, the jingling of bells and the intoxicating scent of mulled wine from a cauldron simmering by the entrance added to the festive air.

Kat set aside her worries, more or less; they lay in the back of her mind like a nagging itch that came and went when least expected.

"I can see that Philippe's distracted and concerned, and the police speak with him regularly," she reported to Andrea and Molly. "But I'm not aware of anything new happening. Having said that, I've been spending a bit more time taking photos and working on my stuff. The only really strange thing is that we have not been to the property on the Cap since we went to Lyon. He also asked me not to go on my own. And he asked me not to talk about it … even to you guys. So I'd better not say another word until it is over. Hopefully that will be sooner than later. I just don't know …"

Whenever she had mentioned the property, Kat had noticed that he would hesitate before he replied. There would be a twitch in the corner of his eye as he looked past her for a second, breaking eye contact. A slight rise in his voice gave away his concern.

Now, at the market, watching Philippe ply his trade and share his knowledge of his cheeses filled her with pride. She admired the care he took arranging the products on his stand, like an artist composing a still life: shades of gold, cream, caramel and copper; pockets of the blackest blue that studded the whitest of Roqueforts, which were displayed next to bleus with their ripples and dots; the grey slivers of ash that pierced the Morbier; chèvres of all sizes, some wrapped in vine leaves, rolled in ash or nestled on straw, others marinating in the finest herb-infused olive oil. Colors, shapes, textures, all displayed in a way that captured eyes and tempted taste buds.

The day she helped with the decorating, he brought home a Vacherin Mont d'Or for her. Made only in the winter months and perfectly timed for the Christmas table, it was packaged in a spruce-wood box to keep it from spreading all over the place.

"Here," said Philippe, handing her a spoon, "you need this to keep it from—how do you say—woozing all over before you spread it. It's another sexy cheese."

"Oozing," Kat corrected with a grin. She loved his mispronunciations and was certain he sometimes made them up for her entertainment. She tasted the cheese and felt a burst of pleasure in her mouth. He laughed when she accused him of having ulterior motives with his "fromage passion." But there was a sensual quality to his voice when he looked at her and spoke about his choices of cheese just for the two them. His eyes became deep pools of ardor and his lips softened at the corners, lush with pleasure.

"Is it the cheese or me that does this to you?" she asked, with a throaty laugh.

Teasing her slightly, he described how this cheese was first crafted in the eighteenth century. "Only milk from cows of the Montbéliard breed is acceptable. They are fed exclusively grass and hay and at an altitude of not less than 700 metres above sea level."

Take me now, she thought, melting inside, as his voice massaged the words with an accent that never lost its appeal to her.

He toasted some country bread and presented some of the cheese at room temperature and some lightly oven baked with garlic cloves. He poured them each a glass of Chardonnay, also from the Jura Mountains.

Spooning cheese on the bread, they fed luscious bites back and forth, gazing into each other's eyes, until kisses began to mix with the cheese and bread, a delicious communion that finally succumbed to lust.

They spread a throw from the sofa on the floor in front of the fire and took time undressing each other, whispering endearments as they caressed in the flickering light. Words of intense desire drew them more deeply into intimacy. Their lovemaking was long and slow.

Minutes away from the daily market, the Christmas market, with its traditional peaked-roof stalls was soon set up around Place Nationale magically transforming the vieille ville. Sparkling strings of lights were hung on the outside of houses throughout the narrow streets, and a small train gave children free rides while their parents browsed the market and sampled foods. The air was filled with the smells of gingerbread, baking apples, mulled wine and apple cider and the strains of festive music. Vendors worked at perfecting their pitches to convince strollers of the need for their holiday wares to ensure plaisir.

"I can't believe that this time last year I was helping my mother prepare for Christmas, and she was helping me to get back on my feet again," Kat said, nostalgia washing over her, as she stopped for a café au lait one morning with Annette.

Annette smiled and raised her espresso cup in a salute. "Yours is a wonderful story. I think it is true love you found in Antibes."

Kat nodded, her eyes flicking past her friend into nothingness for a moment. "I don't think I will ever stop wondering how I settled into the controlling, emotionless marriage I had. To think I never saw it for what it was until I was out of it."

"You aren't the only one, mon amie." Annette's tone of voice implied something more than simple understanding, and it did not go unnoticed by Kat. It wasn't the first time her new friend had hinted at a less than happy marriage, and Kat once spotted nasty bruises on her arms below the sleeves, which Annette had quickly adjusted.

Kat had an uneasy feeling that something might be very wrong, but felt she did not know her well enough yet to inquire. Still, she thought, I'm going to ask her, and soon. I'll take a chance.

Annette had convinced Kat to consider applying for a part-time position in the English-language research department of the company she worked for. Kat was starting to miss working, after having had her own career for almost thirty years before her French adventure began. Her days were busy and full and happy, but she felt the need for some other kind of fulfilment. She had planned to apply for the position in January, but the encouragement of Véronique and the other artists at the workshop in Entrevaux had steered her thoughts in another direction.

She and Philippe chatted about what kind of work she might do from time to time, and she knew she could not work full time. She wanted a few days a week to spend with Philippe and to work with him on the property on the Cap, assuming that he would soon be able to tell her it was all right for her to resume working there.

While she was working on her photography portfolio one evening, her thoughts went back to her conversations with the artists in Entrevaux, and the talks they had about possibilities and dreams. Perhaps she should make her photography her profession.

"You could showcase your photographs and sell prints online, and make beautiful cards," Philippe suggested. "And André recently told me he wants you to hang some of your work in his gallery. He was impressed with your photography and is going to call you."

Kat knew she had an eye. Whether she was taking candid shots or composing a still life, the task of getting it perfectly balanced and framed felt effortless and rewarding. She could spend a lot of time and thought, when she had a particular goal in mind, trying the shot from various angles and at different times of day to see how the light changed it. She had taken courses in studio photography but preferred to work with natural light.

Philippe's excitement mounted. "Think about it. Your time would be your own and you would not be bound to any company's schedule."

"I love the idea," she said. "It just never occurred to me before that I could make my photography my career."

"Pourquoi pas? C'est une idée merveilleuse!"

Kat looked at him as a mischievous smile slowly spread across her face. "How about this?" she said. "A website about cheese and photography?"

Now it was Philippe's turn to look perplexed.

"You always have exotic and entertaining stories about cheese and you have so many customers who come to you with questions, why not put all that on a website?"

"Ha! It's been suggested before but I never gave it any consideration."

"Pourquoi pas?" Katherine said, her head cocked to one side. "I could do the photography."

"And you would have to do an English translation."

"Fromage et Photographie," Katherine tossed out.

"Photographie et Fromage," countered Philippe.

"Fromagegraphie!" they said in chorus. Then they looked at each other in surprise and burst out laughing.

"C'est ça!"

"Seriously," she replied, "I think that's the one."

They raised their glasses of water and toasted the new name.

Kat spoke excitedly. "We can highlight one cheese each week, and if they are crafted nearby we could take a road trip, photograph the cows, goats, sheep, whatever. How much fun would that be? I'll take scenic and artistic shots too. I am loving this idea!"

Philippe was just as enthusiastic. "We can list my inventory, and customers can place their orders online and just stop by the marché to pick it up. Yacht owners in particular would love that. They send their people over with lists to be made up and collected anyway."

"There would be less congestion around your stall on busy days."

Philippe picked Kat up and whirled her around.

"It's falling into place already!"

"We'll need some tech help but that won't be a problem with all the IT companies around here."

Laughing as Philippe set her down, Kat shook her head. "I'm going to get bruises from pinching myself so often."

"Then stop! You're not dreaming. I promise."

Katherine's thoughts turned to her mother frequently during these weeks of Christmas preparations. Her grief at her mother's sudden death was still raw, in spite of all the good things that had come into Kat's life since then. Time doesn't make the hurt of such a loss go away. She was learning to manage the pain but she knew she would always feel heartache mixed with love when she thought of her.

She often stopped abruptly in the midst of what she was doing to consider the complete transition her life had undergone in the short space of six months: a new country, new home, new friends, and a love that was opening aspects of herself she never knew existed.

She now realized that the only planning James and she had done for most of their marriage concerned their bicycle trips. They never talked about their desires or what ambitions one of them might have had. From the beginning, communication was not a strong point between them, and when the passion they shared in the early days began to fade, and eventually disappear, they only had mundane conversations. Both of them had transferred that passion into their careers.

Even though she often felt unhappy in her marriage, she believed she was happy. Nothing was really wrong but nothing was really right. She had accepted her situation as normal and never talked about it with anyone. Not even with Andrea. She saw Molly sporadically during all those years and when they did get together, it was the ongoing drama in Molly's life that needed attention.

The counselor she had finally seen months after James left had helped her realize that their marriage had been in a quietly destructive cycle for many years and quite probably was beyond help. That had helped her come to terms with James' walking out, although it still didn't erase the pain of his betrayal.

She could look at their relationship more clearly now and take some responsibility for the failure. One thing was certain: clear communication was now essential in her life. Lesson learned.

Thinking about the past inevitably led to memories of her family's mouth-watering goulash and paprikash and the laughter that accompanied cooking and baking marathons in the kitchen.

Philippe loved the shortbread she baked recently, insisting on learning how to mix the dough by hand so he could make the cookies himself. "When I was working and studying in England, I tasted very good shortbread," he said, "but none, I repeat, aucun matched your recipe."

Recently they had been spending more time together in the kitchen. Kat wondered if this was related to the worries Philippe had since the explosion.

The atmosphere in the kitchen was relaxed when the work was shared and appreciated. Philippe declared that he ate enough sweets in December to last him the whole year; Kat thought that was probably the case with many people in France. She marveled at the mouth-watering, over the top, displays in the shops: fantastical chocolate creations and pastries she had not seen before. At the daily market and in the local supermarché, displays were packed to bursting with creatively stacked galette des rois, the cake of kings, served on January 6.

One evening, they met with others from the cycling club at a large tent at the market where live Christmas trees, les sapins de Noël, were for sale, many of them with roots so they could be replanted. The fragrance of pine, spruce and cedar filled the air and momentarily swept Katherine back to her childhood, filling her with a deep melancholy.

Philippe noticed she was standing apart and moved quickly to her side.

"Is something wrong?"

Shaking her head, she said, "I was remembering happy times as a child. Choosing the Christmas tree was always a major event for my parents and me. Even though they are both gone, vivid images remain."

His hand on her cheek, Philippe said, "Noël can bring a mix of memories—some happy, some sad. We will make ours beautiful."

"Let's hope nothing interferes with it. I do wish the police would tell us what is happening with the investigation."

"Be patient, Minou. These things take time, as they explained to us."

There had been no trouble since the explosion, and most of the time in the days since their return from Lyon it was easy for Kat to forget there was anything to worry about.

When they rejoined the rest of the group, Katherine said, "I'm glad to see artificial trees haven't become as popular here as in North America."

Laughing and joking, the group took their time choosing perfect trees and then carried them home through the narrow streets.

"No vehicles needed here," Kat said.

She and Philippe had bought bundles of boughs to make a door wreath, branches of holly, and a hand-tied bunch of mistletoe, as well as a tree.

Kat's spirits rose as they began decorating the apartment and the aromatic scent of the boughs wafted into each room. She paused occasionally to watch him work, admiring and appreciating his involvement. James had only ever permitted minimal decorations and had never lifted a finger to help her.

"Next week let's make a wreath for the door of the villa on the Cap. This will help it look beautiful in spite of its condition," Katherine suggested.

Philippe's voice was full of emotion as he drew her to him. "Bonne idée. After all the years it has sat neglected ..."

"Perhaps we will be able to celebrate Christmas there next year," she said. A ripple of desire moved through her as it always did when he held her like that, and she was surprised to feel his body stiffen. He turned away abruptly to fasten another bough, giving her only an unconvincing nod.

He's more worried than he lets on, she realized.

18

A sharp rap on the door late in the afternoon startled Katherine. The building security required a visitor to buzz from the gate to the courtyard and then again in the lobby before gaining access to the elevator or the broad, marble staircase that wound up to the apartments on the upper levels. The French were very good at security.

Kat climbed down from the stepladder where she had been draping boughs over the mirror and had almost reached the door when she heard a key turn in the lock.

For a second, she thought it must be Philippe. But that made no sense. He'd said he was going to be back late today as he and Gilles were going to visit a supplier. Besides, he wouldn't have knocked.

The door opened. An odd couple walked into the entrance hall.

First was a disheveled looking middle-aged man wearing a shiny, rumpled suit that was at least one size too small and an equally ill-fitting toupée. Bushy eyebrows shaded squinty eyes, and his face was overpowered by a large, red-veined nose. From his uneven stubble and a strong smell of garlic emanating from every pore, Kat gathered that personal hygiene was not a priority for him.

The steely gaze of the white-haired, older woman slightly behind him belied her fragile stature and gave Katherine an immediate chill. Her perfectly coifed hair and relatively unlined face spoke of one who spent a great deal of money on her appearance. Still, there was something about her pointed features and icy pale eyes that made her look sinister. She was wearing an expensive-looking, severe black suit that fitted her body as perfectly as her pinched expression.

"Oui?" asked Katherine, more confused than alarmed.

The man spoke in a language she could not understand, but realized later was French with a heavy Russian accent.

"I'm sorry?" Katherine said in English.

"Vee look for Philippe," hissed the man, a gold front tooth glistening, as he switched to broken English not much more than a whisper. The woman glared at Katherine.

"Philippe will not be home until this evening. Who are you? Why do you have a key to this apartment?"

The woman whispered urgently into his ear as the man looked sideways at Katherine, and then he continued, "Vee vish to speak to Philippe. He is not here?"

"Normally he is. But not today. Who are you?"

Katherine stiffened as the unpleasant man approached closer than was socially acceptable, let alone polite, enveloping her in a cloud of foul breath and cheap cologne. He grabbed her arm and pushed her onto the couch.

"I vill look!"

Katherine began to object and get up but stopped when the woman stepped forward, reaching into her handbag and shouting,"Non!" Her eyes narrowed with hostility.

Her imagination racing about what the woman was holding, Katherine stayed where she was as the man searched the apartment. The woman stared, keeping her hand hidden, a tic in her jaw accelerating.

After a minute, the man returned. "Tell him vee not wait longer for answer. He knows!" he snarled. Then he leaned in and poked her sharply on the shoulder. Kat recoiled in revulsion.

"Don't touch me! Who are you?" she demanded.

"Pas important. You tell him vee return," the man snapped.

They turned and strode down the corridor.

Kat was so dumbfounded, she couldn't move for a few minutes. Then she brushed her hair from her eyes and rose to close the heavy door. Adrenalin was rushing through her, making her face flush and her heart pound. She walked back to the couch and slowly sunk into it, then burst into tears. What the hell just happened, she wondered. That disgusting worm had actually assaulted her. How did they have a key and just walk in? Who would do that?

The more she thought about it, the angrier she grew. She came up with all the things she might have said, but didn't think of at the moment. One thing she soon knew for certain was that she had just met Idelle.

"Non!" Philippe shouted minutes later when she called him. "Are you all right?"

"Oui! I'm still shaking though, and I can't stop crying. One minute I'm terrified and the next I'm furious."

He let loose a string of French curses, then said, "I'll be right home. Don't open the door to anyone."

After they hung up, Kat thought, I don't need to open the door for them. They can do it themselves.

Philippe arrived in record time and Kat flew to him for a hug. "I'm so sorry," he said. "Are you OK?"

She held him tightly, even though she was trembling. "I'm OK. I just can't believe what happened. It's like something from a movie now but I was terrified at the time. My imagination was going crazy, and I thought the woman had a gun in her purse."

"Tell me everything. Don't leave out any details."

He nodded as she described the woman. "Zut! Idelle, for sure. A gun? She may well have had one."

The accomplice was unknown to him. "Sounds like one of Dimitri's henchmen. Apparently he has a few."

They sat side by side on the sofa, Philippe's arm around her.

"This may be getting out of hand, Minou," he said, his voice trembling in anger. "I'm furious that they had any contact with you. It should not have happened."

"How did they have a key to get in?"

"I was thinking about that on the way home. Idelle had a key when Viv was ill. I never thought about that after and I never considered changing the locks. Why would I?"

"That makes sense, but you better do it now."

"I called le serrurier on the way here, and he will arrive shortly to do just that. I don't want to say this but, as I've suggested before, perhaps you should go to Toronto for a while until this whole matter is resolved."

"I'm not leaving you."

"Please think about it."

"I'm fine. I will be fine. Surely these people are not that crazy."

"You have no idea," he said, and Kat heard fear in his voice. "I may have to insist."

Within an hour the lock had been replaced with the most secure model available.

With the new lock in place and the security people stationed at the market since the explosion, Kat felt safe as they drove that evening to NouNou restaurant on the beach en route to Cannes. Philippe had said they would counteract this horrible incident by going somewhere extraordinary and meaningful. "We are not going to let these bastards beat us down."

The police had insisted on calling the incident a home invasion, and had made it clear to Katherine that it could have ended very differently. She got the impression they wanted her to be scared, and Philippe continued to fret about her safety.

"I'm not sure about anything now," Philippe said. He was rather dejected, in spite of the exceptional dinner they were enjoying. "We will see what Paris has to say. I'm back to thinking it might be better for all of us if I just walk away and not take these criminals on."

"Please do not do that, I beg you," Kat pleaded. "That property has been in your family for generations. It's your birthright. You've got to fight for it. For the dream we share for it."

"I promise I will do everything in my power to make sure the right thing happens, but we don't know what we are up against just yet. I still think you should leave until it's over."

"How can I leave you now? I want to be by your side, and I will be. Now let's share a crème brûlée and talk about something happy. Before we know it, Adorée will be home and we will all be on our way to Joy's for Christmas. I'm so excited about that."

Philippe look at her adoringly. "I am a lucky man."

"Works both ways, Chouchou."

19

The next day, two police officers came to the apartment to report that their undercover colleagues had noticed Idelle and her companion leaving the apartment building and to apologize for having missed the couple's arrival. Their car had been followed to a gated villa on Cap Ferrat and surveillance was continuing.

Closed circuit television cameras had been placed down in the cove area in the hope that they'd catch some concrete evidence of smuggling. Plans were in place for a sting operation, when the time was right, and they would tell Katherine and Philippe when it was over.

"It would not be wise for you to know any details of this operation, particularly the date and time. Try to carry on as usual."

Kat and Philippe were determined to do just that. And, so, Kat decided that she would keep her promise to meet up with her ex-pat women's group for lunch in Nice that Wednesday. Then Véronique emailed her an invitation for her and Philippe to dine with her and her husband, David, that same evening at their apartment in Nice. "Do you have skates?" she asked. "There's une patinoire in Massena for the holidays."

"I do, but in Toronto, and Philippe doesn't." Katherine wrote back, accepting the invitation.

Véronique told her that they could rent skates at the rink and they would all teach him. "It will be great fun!"

"It will be good to have dinner with Véronique and meet her husband," Philippe said when he heard the plan. "I'm not so sure about the skating lesson. It could be painful."

"Yes, it could. You're a good sport for agreeing to try it."

Philippe muttered something about being crazy rather than a good sport as they fell asleep.

When she kissed Philippe goodbye that morning they arranged to meet at a bar near Place Massena later in the afternoon, before dinner. He hadn't decided whether he would drive in or take the train as Kat was doing. The closer she got to the Nice station, the more Kat looked forward to strolling with her camera through this town, which she loved almost as much as Antibes.

She had left early enough to amble down to the sea before meeting the group, and as she walked, she reveled in the play of light and color in the streets around her, which never failed to entrance her. Sunlight, angling down into the narrow streets, washed over elegant, multi-hued façades, which combined the colors of Italy with the grace of France. Pink, ecru, teal, olive, terra cotta, peach, turquoise, amber: all caught her eye, and from time to time, she stopped to take a photo of a fading pastel shutter or a bold shade of wall. The luminosity of the sea and sky created shades of blue, turquoise and azure unique to this jewel on the coast, Kat thought. Their magic has attracted artists for centuries, and it's so easy to see why.

After meeting up with the women, they walked over to Place Massena. When she caught sight of the Christmas market there, Kat's jaw dropped.

From a distance she had spotted the large ferris wheel, but the big surprise was the extent of the market. There was row upon row of wooden huts with peaked roofs, all decorated individually and offering an enormous selection of wares and food.

The women had no problem spending the entire morning choosing gifts and sampling crêpes, gingerbread and other treats, but the photo ops kept Katherine busier than the shopping, although she did pick up a few items to take along to Joy's at Christmas.

When they stopped for a break in a small café, their conversation soon turned to Kat's decision to remain in France. She appreciated their interest and the openness with which they talked about the obstacles they had discovered as they attempted to assimilate and build their lives here. Absorbing their words, Katherine was reminded there would be challenges ahead.

When it was time for lunch there was consensus they had nibbled on so many treats they could not eat another morsel. Before wishing each other Joyeux Noël, they planned their next meet-up in January, and Kat eagerly noted the date in her calendar.

Strolling up to the Musée Chagall, Kat considered how fortunate she was to be part of such a diverse and welcoming group. She had never contemplated joining such a group when she was caught in the narrow valley of her life with James, and now she was aware of what she had missed for so many years.

The afternoon passed quickly at the gallery, even though she lingered at each piece of art. The impact of the large-scale paintings in the main salon was enhanced by the beauty of the building's simple design.

She was particularly struck by Chagall's homage to love, painted in bursts of passionate reds and pinks in his Song of Songs pieces. Looking at them was a spiritual experience for her now that her heart had been awakened. She had not visited the gallery since she had fallen in love with Philippe.

She wiped away tears more than once as she was drawn into Chagall's celebration of love. The text that accompanied the art, along with the stirring Bach selections on the audioguide, enhanced the magic of the small hexagonal room where the paintings were hung. The evocative images and rich colors were a passionate marriage of the sacred and the sensual. His playful imagery praised the beauty of love and expressed his joie de vivre. Katherine sat there for some time, overwhelmed.

As she made her way back down through the lower part of the Cimiez district, heading toward Place Massena, she felt like she was floating on a cloud—until she became aware that someone was following her.

There had been a constant stream of pedestrians at first, so she had not noticed anything. Now, as she approached the busier streets under an overpass, she definitely had a sense of being shadowed. She had been looking around carefully before she crossed busy streets, and twice she caught a glimpse of someone ducking into a doorway or stopping to examine something on the ground. As much as she wanted to blame her imagination, she suddenly felt frightened.

On avenue Jean Médecin, the main shopping street, a longer sideways glance when she paused to look in a store window told her she was being followed by Idelle's loathsome companion.

Her pulse quickened. Something that felt like panic played with her thoughts for a moment as she considered what to do. Then she pulled out her phone, attempting to appear nonchalant.

Philippe was alarmed when she told him. "I will come to meet you right now," he said. "Was he around all morning?"

"He wasn't in the musée because it was very quiet there today. I would have noticed him. How did he find me? Why is he doing this? What should I do?"

"Keep walking. I am already on my way. Try not to worry. I'll call Thibideau to alert him about this."

"Well, if the police are doing their job, he should already know."

The street was busy now with pedestrians, and Kat began to feel calmer each time she looked around. She decided to play a game with her stalker by speeding up then slowing down, and stopping to look at window displays. She was determined to make his task as annoying as possible.

Her imagination raced as she considered turning into the enormous Nice Étoile shopping centre and seeing if she could ditch him. Then she wondered if whoever was watching her was watching him now too.

Philippe called back after a few minutes.

"They are on it, Kat. They're watching him—and you. Thibideau said not to worry but he wants me to just wait at the bar, as we first planned. He suspects they are following you to find me, so I'm turning around now. You'll be here soon. Reste calme."

Kat described the game she was playing as she walked and laughed, a little nervously. Philippe failed to see the humor, and his voice echoed his concern. "Minou, just be careful. It's not a game."

"Well now that I know he's being watched, it almost feels like one. I'm not going to make it easy for him."

Philippe asked her about the rest of her day and, happily engaged in conversation with him, Kat barely noticed when she turned onto one side street and then another. Still, she let out a sigh of relief as she shut her phone and stepped into Les Brasseries Georges, where Philippe was waiting.

He kissed Kat's cheeks gently before her hands went to his face, and her lips delivered a passionate kiss that took him by surprise.

"That kind of kiss does not happen in public very often," he laughed. "To what do I owe the pleasure?"

She pulled him close and whispered that the kiss was thanks to Marc Chagall's art. Then she added that Idelle's repugnant companion had still been behind her as she turned down the street to the bar. "Hold me close and look over my shoulder. Can you spot him?"

He looked through the front window and saw the man she had described being frisked by police. "Mon Dieu! He does look vile. They have caught him already and have him up against a car. It must be an unmarked police car."

He held on to her tightly, reporting what he was seeing, until his cellphone rang. As he answered it, he pulled out a chair for Kat at the bar. She sat down and took a long swig of his pastis.

"That was Thibideau," he said when he joined her. "We are to stay in Nice tonight and not go back to Antibes."

Kat was feeling relieved to be with Philippe, but she still thought that this was a wise idea. A minute later, after a nod from Philippe, a waiter led them to a quiet corner of the bar, where they settled on a soft leather banquette and tried to collect themselves. Philippe ordered her a pastis and then called the Hotel Beau Rivage, a quick walk from there on La Prom, to make a reservation.

"This is turning into quite a date night," he said. "I'll call Gilles right now to let him know he'll be opening the shop tomorrow."

Now she was safe, the scare she'd had caught up with her and her hand shook as she picked up her glass. She said, "You know, part of me wanted to confront that sleazy guy and give him a swift kick! I really felt I could do it."

Philippe was angry that Kat had been targeted once again. He fumed for several minutes before she convinced him she was fine and thankful the police were doing their job. "Maybe this means the situation will be all over with soon," she said.

"Every time I think about this, I have to shake my head. I still find it hard to believe that we are involved with drug dealers. There are moments when it's frightening and others when it seems like we are dealing with petty thieves. It's quite a roller coaster."

After some conjecture as to what the police were doing, Kat changed the topic completely. Placing her fingers lightly on Philippe's cheek, she described her emotional response at the museum.

"It was magical, truly magical, thanks to the love you have brought into my life."

"The next time we will go together—and not have it spoiled like today."

At 7:00 p.m., they rang the bell to Véronique and David's pied-à-terre in the old town and then climbed the steep stairs to the second floor. They still felt somewhat shaken about everything, but were looking forward to the evening.

"It will be just the diversion we need," Kat said.

"I'm not certain I'm looking forward to the skating," Philippe said, shooting her an accusatory look. "Whose bright idea was that?"

Kat said nothing. She was too busy looking around the ancient stairwell. "What character! It's just like their place in Entrevaux—mysterious and intriguing."

Philippe laughed, "To me it's just another old building in need of repair, but to you it's magical. I like that."

Véronique greeted them, with her husband close behind. David extended his hand to Philippe and bised Katherine.

"I've been looking forward to meeting you both," he said, his friendly voice booming as he took their coats. "Welcome to our humble abode."

They were in a large drawing room with fifteen-foot ceilings, elaborate crown moldings and three sets of French doors across in one wall that lead out to a terrace. The room functioned as a living–dining area and there was an elegantly screened alcove to one side, which Véronique told them was their sleeping area. Kat could see no sign of a kitchen.

Standing at an ornately carved bar tucked in one corner, David filled champagne flutes that Katherine recognized as the distinctive Biot glassware she was collecting. He set them on a tray beside bite-size toasts topped with foie gras, and added a small bowl of Niçoise olives.

"How does this sound?" he asked in a voice that still betrayed his Boston roots. "We'll go skating first and then come back for dinner."

"Speaking of dinner," Kat said, "Where on earth do you cook here?"

Véronique was clear in her response, "I don't."

David laughed and nodded. "She's not allowed to cook! It's a family rule … although she certainly pitched in when the children were young. Make no mistake! But really it is my domain. Look."

He led them to a panel on the far side of the room, that turned out to be a pocket door. He opened the door to reveal the smallest yet best-equipped galley kitchen imaginable.

"I just keep the panel open when we are here alone and ... voilà ... as good a kitchen as anywhere. When we have company, it simply disappears."

Kat expressed her amazement at the versatility of design used in transforming the centuries-old spaces. "There are always surprises!" She hoped the day would come soon when she and Philippe would have their chance and refused to believe the dream would die.

They chatted easily for a while before heading out. Philippe gently squeezed Kat's hand when he noticed her looking around nervously. "I'm sure everything is fine now, chérie. We are in good hands."

Kat found it hard to quell her anxiety as they walked to Place Massena. But they were soon lacing up skates under the twinkling fairy lights strung around the ice rink, and her mood lightened. The squeals of delight from skaters and spectators of all ages filled the air.

Kat and Philippe rented their skates, while Véronique and David had their own.

"Skating is something we have done as a family since David first taught me in America," Véronique explained. "He still plays hockey once a week with 'the guys' in an ex-pat league where you have to be over sixty years old."

"We started playing together when we were all in our thirties," David said. "We've lost a few along the way but most have hung in. It's an addictive sport."

"When they began playing hockey, they called themselves the Yankee Clippers –"

David interrupted, with a loud chuckle, "And now we are the Yankee Old Farts."

Philippe looked puzzled, and Véronique told David he would have to do the explaining, which he did, accompanied by much laughter from the others.

"I have a confession," Philippe told them. "I have never been on skates before."

Kat was surprised "You didn't say 'never' before."

Flashing her a grin, he confidently stepped onto the ice. He had barely finished saying "On y va!" when his feet slipped in different directions and, arms flailing, he fell on his butt.

Kat burst into laughter. Unable to stop, she barely made it to the railing around the rink and came perilously close to falling herself. After David helped him up, Philippe steadied himself beside her.

"I'm sorry," she gulped, between snorts. "Are you OK? I should have warned you … and I shouldn't be laughing … but …"

Philippe was laughing too.

Brushing off his jeans, he said. " I thought I could just step out on the ice and glide off. Mon Dieu! My feet were completely out of control."

David gave him a few tips about how to stay vertical, then the two women each took one of his arms and they slowly began again.

The threesome came close to collapsing in a heap a few times, as Philippe's slipping and sliding threw them all off balance, but gradually he began to get the feel of it.

They skated for an hour in the festive ambiance of the area. The large ferris wheel glowed like an enormous Christmas decoration, and the lineup to ride on it was steadily lengthened by people who had finished sauntering through the market area. The now familiar aromas of mulled wine and roasting chestnuts filled the air. The air was crisp, but the temperature was above freezing and skating kept them warm.

Kat and Philippe soon were able to skate together, with just the odd wobble. David and Véronique glided around, arm in arm, their affection obvious as they paused from time to time under a mistletoe bunch.

The two couples stopped at an espresso bar before strolling back to the apartment for an appetizing coq au vin, which Véronique wholly credited to her husband.

Over dinner, David entertained them with tales of Véronique's early days in the States, when they were first dating, and then followed up with stories about his transition to living in France.

"Katherine, you need to know that starting over in a new country with a foreign language to master isn't always going to be easy. No matter how much in love you are with Philippe and France, be prepared for some challenges and always, I repeat, always maintain your sense of humor."

"I had the same issues to deal with during the years I spent in America," Véronique said. "That's the price we pay for these amorous adventures—but look at the rewards."

On that note David and Philippe high-fived and they all decided it was time to call it a night.

The pleasure of the evening began to fade even as Kat and Philippe strolled the few blocks to the hotel. The distraction had been welcome, but now their thoughts turned back to the menace they were facing and their mood became somber as they speculated about what might be happening.

"Let's hope it all ends soon," Kat said. Philippe was grimly silent.

20

At 7:00 the next morning, Philippe's cellphone rang. It was Inspecteur Thibideau. From Kat's perspective, the call consisted of Philippe nodding his head and saying only a few words.

When he hung up, he said, "Ça marche—there's been some progress. Arresting the guy you refer to as "the slimeball" paid off. He's a little minnow in a large pond, and to save his own skin he confirmed what the police already suspected. As you say, he sang like un oiseau—a bird, oui? They could not have asked for better luck. Now they can proceed with the plan they have been working on for a while."

"I can't believe it," Kat said. "I just can't believe we are involved in this. But what would they charge him with when he was just following me?"

"Apparently they discovered he had drugs on his person. I have an idea the police had something to do with putting them there, but that's just a guess."

Kat shook her head. "Unbelievable."

"Curiously," Philippe said, "someone on the Cap is helping them with the surveillance of the cove. That would mean someone is on or near our property. Imagine! Thibideau wants to see us to talk about it, and a driver is waiting outside now. I'm sorry."

He had been pacing the room as he spoke but now sat beside her on the bed and took her hand. "You will have to identify Monsieur Slimy in a lineup. Is that upsetting?"

Kat flopped back on the pillows. "Unbelievable! Incroyable!"

Philippe pulled her up and hugged her tightly. "We will have our lives back before too long. "

Kat left his arms and moved over to the window, threw open the shutters and hollered to the world, "We will have our lives back again! Philippe promised!"

Turning to Philippe, she said, "I needed to do that just to believe what you said is true. I can't help feeling we're in a movie. "

Philippe nodded. "It's only been six weeks since they left the note, but it seems like forever. What we didn't know is that this investigation has been going on for years. They just couldn't get a fix on Dimitri after he and Idelle left their home in the north, until we got in on the act. It's going to be interesting to hear what the Inspecteur has to tell us."

"I keep wondering how this kind of drama—and danger—can happen to people who have what we think of as normal lives. But I know it does, only too well. Molly's brother was involved with drugs and a lot of very sketchy characters for years."

Philippe nodded. "You told me all about that and Molly's futile commitment to helping him."

"And do you remember me mentioning Lucy, a friend in Toronto from my former job?"

Philippe nodded again.

"One time she was off work for a few days. When she returned, she told us that one of her cousins had been involved in an Asian gang—there are a few of them in Toronto—and ended up being shot to death. Her entire family was under investigation for weeks and it was, for her, simply surreal. He had seemed to be a quiet university student. No one knew he was a major player in the gang."

"It happens these days. "

Kat took his hand and kissed his palm. "I know this is much more intense for you, because you have to protect Adorée. I'm so sorry it ever happened."

"I am the one to apologize," he said. "I'm sorry that you are involved in this. You've seen me at my worst at times because of it." His sad expression and emotion-charged words brought Kat to the brink of tears.

"Then that's a good thing," she assured him, hoping to lighten the air. "If this is your worst, I'm certain I can deal with it. I could say the same about me. I definitely am having awful moments from time to time."

Philippe swallowed hard and shook his head at her words. His look conveyed all he wanted her to know.

They sat silently for a few moments until Philippe remembered that a car and driver was waiting for them. They quickly showered and dressed.

Walking straight through the lobby and out to the sidewalk, as instructed, Katherine squeezed Philippe's hand and murmured, "Just keep me close."

He squeezed back.

A black SUV was waiting, its motor running, and a solidly-built middle-aged man in an equally black suit held open the back door for them. He spoke rapid French as they climbed in and Philippe translated.

"He apologized, but the windows are blacked out, so we will not be able to see where we are going."

Kat nodded, her eyes wide.

The vehicle stopped in an underground garage, and they were immediately ushered into an elevator and then to an office, where Inspecteur Thibideau rose to greet them. Kat was aware of a distinctive smell of strong tobacco in his presence. His manner was professional and to the point. After thanking them for their assistance with this "criminal issue," he explained to Katherine that they hoped she could help by identifying the suspect in a lineup.

He called for an officer to escort her to the room from where she would view a number of men from behind a mirrored window. Trying hard to appear calm and collected, she waved to Philippe and left the room. She was certain she would have no problem identifying the man who had scared her so badly.

She followed the officer through a labyrinth of hallways and glass doors that silently opened and closed as they made their way. They stopped in a small room with no chairs and a two-way mirror.

"Madame Price, you will see six men walk onto the low platform where they will turn to face this way. Please take your time and do not respond until you are completely certain which man you wish to identify. This is most important."

A few minutes later, Kat's stomach tensed with nerves, as the six men mounted the platform and stood in profile. All of them were around the same height and weight, but two of them were bald and one had very curly hair. Three of them clearly had not shaved, and one had a full beard.

Kat looked intently at their stature and at their clothes, which ranged from dirty jeans and T-shirts to a tailored suit. She was surprised that she could not immediately tell who had been following her. Then the officer spoke into an intercom, and the six men, numbers hanging around their necks, turned to face her.

She recognized him now: standing second from the right and wearing the same scowl he had both times he had come into her life. The toupée and nose were unmistakable, even though his clothes were completely different.

The officer escorted her back through the maze of corridors to Philippe and Inspecteur Thibideau, her job done.

Thibideau thanked her for her help and said, "We will continue to have our undercover operatives watch you both at all times until this matter is resolved. But I cannot divulge any information regarding dates or time. We need to maintain the utmost secrecy. I will just say that it is necessary for us to move very quickly. Of course, you will not visit your property on the Cap until after we speak again. I cannot stress enough how important it is that you stay away. In all other ways, please carry on as usual."

Their curiosity was piqued once again when he added, "A most reliable operative is helping us in a very sensitive way that will ensure we succeed, and soon."

With that, he rose, shook their hands and buzzed for yet another officer to accompany them to the exit.

They arrived back at their apartment mid-morning, and after changing his clothes, Philippe went straight to work. Kat decided she needed a quiet day at home. After all the worry of the preceding weeks, a long soak in a bubble-filled tub was in order.

It was unusual for her to spend an entire morning at home. She had established a rhythm of sorts to her days, one that was dictated by choice rather than deadlines imposed by a job. It felt lovely to luxuriate in the bath, but as soon as she dried herself and dressed, she felt a surge of anxiety as the events of the past twenty-four hours replayed in her mind. All this stress and worry was so unlike her normal state. Her usual it-will-all-work-out attitude had been pushed to the limit, and not being able to talk about it with Molly and Andrea had removed the safety valve for her fears.

She settled into the window seat and opened her iPad to a novel by one of her favorite authors. As much as she tried to lose herself in the story of a teenage boy who steals a painting, her mind kept wandering. She was glad of the interruption when the cellphone vibrated on the table.

"Bonjour, chérie!"

"Bonjour, Simone! How lovely to hear from you. How are you?"

"I'm calling to ask if you might drop by today. I hope you don't mind."

"I'm flattered, Simone. Truly."

"I would like to treat you to lunch. À treize heures?"

"Lovely! I'll see you at one o'clock. May I bring something with me?"

"Rien du tout, merci. I have all I need. Do you like escargots, snails?"

"If you had asked me five months ago, I would have said no. But now I am a fan."

On her way to Simone's, Katherine stopped by the market to tell Philippe about the invitation.

"So thank you for those delicious meals of fresh escargots you've treated me to these past few months."

"Zut! That was another little gastronomic hurdle you had to cross. I remember the look on your face the first time I put them on the table."

Kat nodded. "I was sure I would hate the taste and the consistency, and I was so wrong. I wonder how she will prepare them."

He looked at her intently then led her to a quiet spot, leaving Gilles to handle the lineup of customers. "Are you okay? You seem to be trying very hard to be relaxed and chatty."

Kat blinked and nodded. "You're right. I'm working on it, but I'm okay, honest, and I always feel good when I visit Simone. She's so calming. I'll be just fine by the time you see me later today."

Philippe put his arms around her. "Yes, you will. I know that. You are the calm in my life, Minou, and I thank you for that."

He returned to serving customers and Kat left, reassured that she was loved and appreciated by the man she trusted with her heart. She could almost hear Andrea saying, "Remember, Kat, whatever the problem, it will all work out."

Katherine walked up the driveway to Simone's house carrying a bunch of carrots in one hand and a bright winter bouquet in the other. Near the house, she noticed a thin, leather case, barely larger than a business card, lying by the edge of the driveway, and picked it up. Inside was an embossed crest and a card identifying Detective Guillaume Beaufort.

She slipped it into her pocket and was debating whether to mention it to Simone, when she opened the door. She was leaning on her cane and smiling broadly in welcome.

"Bonjour, Simone! Ça va?"

"Oui, oui, chérie! No wheels today!"

Katherine held out the flowers, which Simone graciously accepted, then she held up the carrots. "I'm just going to slip around the back for a minute. I haven't seen Eeyore, ah, Victor, in over a week."

"Come through here. It's easier to go out the back door to the yard than it is to go around. Everything is so overgrown at the side of the house."

Once she was back outside, Katherine looked down the sloping garden, past the remnants of a vineyard, a few rows of olive trees and a large patch of dried brown sunflower stalks. The end of the property was heavily wooded, with no apparent view to the sea. Looking across to Philippe's property, she could just make out the chimney and the ridge of part of the roof. She wondered if Simone ever ventured down to the sea at the bottom of her property—to the cove. It was unlikely. It wouldn't be possible for her now. The terrain was too rough and the slope to the sea probably too steep.

The donkey trotted over when she called him and nuzzled her arm, too polite to simply grab the carrots. "Ah, burrito, I know what you want," she said as she scratched between his ears. He snuffled with contentment and happily ate her gift.

With her back to Simone, Katherine put her hand on the leather ID case. She wrestled with her thoughts for a moment and made her decision. It was always better to be honest and up front.

"He is as happy to see you as am I, chérie," Simone said from the doorstep, as Katherine came back into the house. "He was bobbing his head at you. That's his happy move."

"Then this will be my happy move back," Katherine replied, turning back and bobbing her head to the donkey. As she looked at the ground for a moment, she was stunned to see a small pile of dark unfiltered cigarette butts neatly gathered by a rock at the side of the path.

Simone motioned her into the large salon. There were several large wicker baskets on the floor that had not been there on earlier visits. Kat took the ID from her pocket and showed it to Simone.

"This was lying at the edge of your driveway."

Simone's jaw twitched slightly, but her demeanor remained relaxed.

Simone took the leather case, then, without looking at it, sat down and patted the cushion beside her. "Sit down with me, chérie. We had a commotion last night in the woods near the sea. The police came to my house, and two very fine officers spent the evening here, even after I went to bed. They were such gentlemen, and very handsome, I might add."

"What was going on?" Kat asked.

Simone gave her a straightforward look. "Do you know, I did not ask. They were not forthcoming, but they assured me they were here to make certain I was safe. Really, that's all I cared about. I do not have time to worry about other matters. As long as they are being taken care of by other people, that's all that's important to me. Perhaps I will hear about it on the news. Perhaps not."

"Obviously someone dropped this. Shall I make some calls and arrange to return it?" Kat reached out to take the ID back.

Responding just a touch too quickly, Kat thought, Simone assured her she would make the call, and she held on to the leather case. There was a surprisingly emphatic tone to her voice that indicated the matter was not open to discussion.

For a moment Kat considered that perhaps Simone was the police's secret helper. Then she decided she was letting her imagination run wild. How could Simone be involved when she could barely walk? Inspecteur Thibideau had told Kat not to discuss anything with anyone. If the police were taking steps to ensure Simone was not affected by what they were doing, so much the better. She had no doubt it was all connected.

Kat's gaze wandered the room. A large hearth with a massive log mantle made a dramatic statement against the white walls and white painted stone of the fireplace. As in the studio, all the furniture was painted or upholstered in white. The only colorful things in the room were the bright throw cushions and the rugs scattered on the terra cotta tiles.

"What a spectacular mantle." Kat got up to take a closer look.

"Oui! C'est un beau manteau de cheminée. It was carved from an old cherry tree on the property that used to have the most spectacular blossoms. We used to lie down on blankets beneath it and pretend the world was a beautiful place." Her eyes took on a faraway look, and Kat supposed that she had been transported back there by her memory. Then Simone blinked and returned to the present. "Look carefully, you can see initials carved into it."

Katherine found two sets, S.G. + G.D. and J-L.G. + O.R, and rubbed her fingers over the second.

"That is Jean-Luc and Olivier," Simone said. "The first summer they met we came here for August, as Parisians do."

Kat moved her hand to the first set, but Simone said not a word about it.

"Bon! This is where we—I mean you—can set up the crèche, if you still would like to do so. I will be able to see everything but I can't reach up to place all the santons."

"I am happy to do this for you, Simone, and I can't wait to see your collection."

As Kat unpacked the wicker baskets, which were full of Christmas decorations and unwrapped the clay santons, Simone told her stories, as if her memories were also being unwrapped.

She had been raised on a dairy farm in Normandy, near Bayeux, she said, where hard work was just part of normal life. Her family produced milk, cheese and butter that was sold at their local co-operative.

"We were known for the rich flavor of our butter. Papa said it was because Maman had a magic touch with the churn and recited poetry as she worked. Maman said it was because the cows were so content eating the sweet grasses and herbs in our meadows while Papa sang to them. They would tease and argue about this all the time. In those days, people took great pride in what they produced and helped each other as a matter of course."

"How delightful," Katherine murmured, picturing it all.

"We were happy, chérie. That is my strongest memory: We were happy."

Simone was the youngest, with three older brothers. When the German occupation began, their life changed dramatically and her father's health began to decline.

"You cannot imagine how our world was destroyed. The German soldiers made us give them most of our products for nothing. My brothers would hide a separate stash that we shared with neighbors as best we could. It was not long before food was scarce and my brothers, in desperation, secretly slaughtered a cow in the middle of the night. This was discovered, and the Germans took my oldest brother away because he insisted he had done it all on his own. I will never forget the look in his eyes as he stared at us to be quiet. We never saw him again."

Katherine had to remind herself to continue unwrapping santons and put them on the mantle.

"I am certain my father had his first heart attack the night they took Marcel away. He was never the same and grew very weak."

Simone described how she and her brothers tried to keep the farm running as well as possible.

"There was never enough food and fuel, and we were often cold and hungry. The Germans forbade us to go anywhere unless we had a special pass, so it became difficult to share anything with neighbors or help each other in any way. We stopped going to school but our mother made certain we read every book in the house and even over again before we had to burn them to keep warm. She would read to my father for hours to distract him from his misery and despair. It's the only way to escape the brutality for at least a few moments, she would tell us."

She paused and looked at the scene Katherine was creating on the mantle. "Merci, chérie. You are making this old lady very happy and unlocking doors I have kept closed for a long time."

Pointing, she said, "The santon of the woman churning butter, that is one my father gave my mother before I was born. The farmer with the cow at his side is one my mother gave him at the same time. The woman sitting in the chair reading is the first one I gave my mother when we put up the crèche again, in Paris, many years after the war."

She went on to point out others that represented her brothers and other meaningful people or circumstances. Her vivid descriptions of village life made the farming community in Normandy come alive in Kat's imagination.

"Simone, you paint images with your words just as you do on your canvases," she said. "You need to record your story so it doesn't get lost. I could help you."

"Ah, oui. You are right. Let's do it together in the new year."

Katherine made a mental note not to forget her promise.

Simone was suddenly wide-eyed. "But I invited you for lunch and we have eaten nothing," she said.

Kat smiled. "Listening has been so much better than eating."

With the help of her cane, Simone stood up. "Come to the kitchen where I have everything ready. It's a simple meal. We can finish the crèche later or another time if you have to go."

Simone asked her to put a covered pottery dish in the pre-heated oven for fifteen minutes. The dish was still warm from whatever preparation occurred earlier.

A simple salad of greens was sitting in a bowl on the table, and Simone tossed it with her homemade vinaigrette.

Katherine was surprised to see an obviously fresh baguette on an olivewood cutting board.

Noticing the look, Simone explained. "I don't eat bread as often as I used to, but when I do, Nathalie at Le Palais du Pain in the market has one of the young men deliver it on his bike. Her grandmother was a good friend of mine. She taught Nathalie all of her baking secrets."

Soon the timer rang on the stove. Kat pulled the dish out and took off the cover to reveal escargots inside large mushroom caps surrounded by a white wine sauce and covered with cheese. She could smell garlic and tarragon in the sauce.

They sat down to eat, and Katherine savored every morsel.

"It's an old, favorite recipe," Simone said. "I'm sure Philippe has brought the same snails from Gaston at the market. They are from Normandy—the best. Jean-Luc called them the Kobe beef of snails. And the mushrooms are local."

"And delicious," Kat said.

They chatted over their food and wine, finishing the meal with a tarte au citron meringuée that Simone had made that morning. "I still like to cook and bake and it's a pleasure to have someone to share it with."

"Simone, I don't mean to be nosy but how do you manage on your own? You seem to have everything you need."

"My roots here are long and deep here, chérie, and now it is the children and grandchildren of my old friends and shopkeepers who help out. Thank goodness Antibes is still a town of small businesses that have stayed in families for generations. It's something that is disappearing quickly in France. Quel dommage. What a pity.

"Monsieur Rousseau delivers from the market on Fridays. I email him my list. My needs are few. His wife, Madame Rousseau, I have never used their first names, just like in the old days, she comes with him and stays for two hours to clean. He comes by to pick her up after his deliveries. They are kind and thoughtful and do not pry. I like that."

"So you have a computer. That's very good."

"Yes, Jean-Luc had one of the first and was adamant that I learn how to use one. I understood quite easily as my job involved electronics. Oh, I didn't get that far in my story, did I? Eh bien, for another day!"

Katherine was shocked when she checked her watch and saw it was already almost 4:00 p.m.

"Désolée! I have kept you from your afternoon rest. The hours just flew by. Shall I finish with the santons?"

"Non, non, chérie. Away you go. You have made a wonderful display as it is."

"Would you like me to come back tomorrow and finish?"

"Only if you wish."

Kat had said not a word about what had happened to her the previous night. However, she had the sense that Simone already knew all about it. There was just something in the look she gave Katherine when she gave her the leather ID case. Perhaps it would all come out in time.

That evening Kat made another batch of shortbread cookies and attempted to keep a few to give away.

"Mon Dieu, these are sinful," Philippe said. "You could set up shop selling these."

Kat popped another in her mouth. "They are addictive, but I want to save some to take to Simone. I'm going to go back tomorrow to finish putting up her santons. She seemed so delighted to see them."

"Tu es gentille, Minou. You are being so kind to this woman."

"I like her a lot. She's so thoughtful and interesting and alive. I know from the childhood stories she told me that she is ninety-four. Imagine! Still living on her own, and painting and cooking. I love it!"

"I can't stop thinking about her telling you the police were at her house yesterday. I agree with you though, they were probably just warning her that they would be keeping an eye on the cove. I'd give anything to know what they are really doing."

"I don't want to know. I just want it to be over."

"Has she told you yet how she knows me?"

"We only got as far as the early years of the German occupation in Normandy this week. Her stories are mesmerizing. I know there must be a lot more to come because she mentioned briefly before that she was in the Resistance."

"Hmm. Grand-père was a maquisard. I wonder if she knew him."

"Well I can't wait for the next chapter, so don't eat all those cookies. Perhaps I will hear more tomorrow."

As it happened, Kat had to rush through her visit to Simone the following day.

Philippe's friend, André, who owned the photography gallery, had called that morning and invited her to come by with her portfolio.

When she told Simone, their talk turned to the subject of art, and Simone was the one asking questions. They exchanged ideas and opinions about their creative approaches and philosophy, while Kat finished setting up the crèche, and Simone's life story did not progress.

"Vraiment, Katherine, I did not expect to enjoy this again, so I am most pleased to look at all the pieces and remember."

"What will you do for Christmas?"

"I will be here alone, as I have been for almost ten years."

"But –" Katherine began.

"Attends, chérie. Listen to me and try to understand. Until ten years ago, my very dear friend Margaux lived here too. Now I am fine in my solitude. I am at peace. I prefer to be alone with my music and my paints—and Victor Hugo, of course—rather than be surrounded by people who are celebrating and are feeling sorry for me. C'est normal."

Kat felt a pang of sadness for her and sensed that Simone knew it.

As if to banish that sentiment, Simone continued, her voice strong and upbeat, "When I moved here after the accident. I had the entire house painted white, as you see it. For me, it represented a tabula rasa, a clear slate, and that is how I begin every day."

Katherine realized that she needed to temper her desire to help with respect for Simone's wishes. She would let Simone set the pace for their friendship. The more time they spent together, the more Katherine became aware of a faintly mysterious edge to her. The words not being said were becoming louder.

Later, as she made her way through the narrow streets to André's studio, excitement about meeting him and what they would talk about bubbled through her and put an extra bounce in her step. She oscillated between feeling anxious at the thought of revealing her relationship with her camera and the images she captured and feeling excited to talk openly about what photography meant to her, as she had with Véronique and the others in Entrevaux.

Until now, she had always considered her photography to be a hobby: a way of expressing her ideas without pointed criticism from James. She hadn't even shown him half of her work through the years they were together.

The thought of embracing her "natural artistry," as André had said to Philippe, and making photography her focus—she smiled to herself at the pun—pleased her immensely.

21

It was over almost as quickly as it had begun.

Monsieur Slimy, as he would forever be known to Kat, had been arrested and charged with drug trafficking, as had another twelve people. The police were confident they had all the top players of Dimitri's gang in the south of France in custody after co-ordinated raids over the previous thirty-six hours. Inspecteur Thibideau, who arrived at Kat and Philippe's apartment at 6:00 a.m. to deliver the news in person, assured them that the police's sting operation was over. Done. Fini.

"Naturellement—of course, I cannot divulge the details," he said and then went on to explain that the cove was not the only location targeted that night. His sources had reported that this gang had already moved most of their operation to the Eastern Europe and Asian markets. They had done their damage in France and were gone. Idelle had not been captured, and the police had reason to believe she had fled ahead of the raids to rejoin Dimitri.

"What was left here were small potatoes for them. We'll probably never catch Dimitri," he said, his mouth twisted in a caustic smile. "Our best guess is that he and Idelle are mixing with the high-rollers on the Russian Riviera, who always protect their own. That brash attitude of hiding in plain sight is frustrating but c'est la vie. We've done what we could here. I don't think you will hear anything from either one of them again. My understanding is that their intent was to scare you off using your property at the Cap, and that was all. The secluded cove at the foot of your property and the one next to you, served them well. It seems it was also, in some warped way of thinking, more about Idelle not wanting to relinquish her hold on you."

Excusing himself to Kat and explaining he wanted to be certain Philippe understood the details, he and Philippe spoke at length in French while Kat tried to follow along.

Finally, the two men stood and shook hands. Thibideau took Katherine's hand, bowing over it as she thanked him for keeping them safe and up to date with all the information, and for coming to speak with them so soon. Her nose wrinkled faintly as the now expected air of strong tobacco lingered.

He blinked rapidly as he explained that he was already in the neighborhood, so it was no inconvenience.

After he left, Kat and Philippe danced together around the apartment for a minute or two in pure joy. They were both enormously relieved. Idelle's mission to scare them had worked but, in the end, right had triumphed. They were curious why he had been in their neighborhood so early in the morning, but soon let that go.

Now they could get on with life. They made a plan to spend the evening looking at restoration drawings for the villa on the Cap that Philippe had stashed away when the trouble began. They had already decided they would like to open a charming inn on the property.

"Let's begin by making lists of our ideas, Minou. This is our future we are planning. Our dream. Our promise to each other."

The continuous stream of festivities delighted Kat. It was such a relief for her simply to enjoy them and not worry about what might unexpectedly happen. She spent much of her days with her camera, capturing small details and moments of unexpected beauty. In the evenings, she selected the best of those shots and worked on her computer to perfect them. Some she put in her daily album, others she set aside for the website, and yet others she put in a folder of candidates to be printed and framed.

Antibes was dazzling in the days before Christmas. Up the street from their apartment, in Place de Gaulle, the fountains were illuminated and spectacular laser shows and light displays enlivened the square at night. The harbor filled with ships for the Semaine de Noël celebrations in the port, and anchored yachts were wreathed with ropes of colored lights and flags, some of them with the figure of Père Noël waving from their masts.

The free commune of Safranier was abuzz with special activities. This medieval village at the heart of Antibes was one of Kat's favorite spots. Its narrow streets, lined with stone houses, led to a square where the community was devoted to maintaining the ancient traditions of this part of France.

Annette rushed Katherine into the square one morning, after yoga.

"Voilà! The longest bûche de Noël in the world. Everyone in the commune bakes cake rolls and brings them here. Then they place them end to end and ice the giant cake before they serve it. This one is more than two metres long."

They sipped thé au citron as they took in the fun and inhaled the delicious aromas of cake and roast chestnuts. Kat hated the taste of the nut, but she loved the smell of them roasting on a brazier.

Katherine stopped by to see Simone one last time before Christmas, bearing a brightly wrapped box full of her shortbread and a small wooden crate of cheeses selected by Philippe. Kat had called her a few days earlier but Simone had asked her not to come then as she was not feeling well. Katherine worried about her but Simone had refused her suggestion that she call every day. "Non, merci. I can make a call if I need to, but I don't want anyone checking on me daily. That would make me feel old!" That morning Simone had left a message to drop by if she had time.

A note on the door read "Entrez," so Katherine let herself in. Dylan's *Blowin' In the Wind* floated down the hallway from the studio.

"Simone! Je suis là!"

"Viens ici! Come down here."

Kat was relieved to see her friend was looking well.

"Bonjour, chérie! I have missed you!"

"Moi aussi! I was concerned about you."

"Really, I was fine, just, as they say, under the weather. L'infirmière came by and confirmed I didn't have pneumonia. That was all I needed to know."

"And you've been painting, I see." An easel was standing under a skylight, its back to the door.

"Oui! It fills me with purpose. It's the best medicine. You awakened my joie de Noël, and I picked this amaryllis from the garden to use as my subject."

She wiped her hands on her smock, which was covered in smudges and streaks of reds and greens, before leaning in to greet Katherine.

"You already look very festive in that smock," Katherine joked.

"My chemise ends up as a work of art by the time I complete a piece," Simone replied, grinning and slipping it off. She hung it on a hook on the wall and wiped the paint off her hands with a rag that stank of turpentine.

Kat looked at the painting on the easel. "This is going to be spectacular," she exclaimed.

"I'm experimenting with a new blend of reds. C'est magnifique, non?"

Beside the easel was a chair on a raised stand.

"That's my throne," Simone said. "I sit in my wheelchair to paint the lower part and climb up to the throne to reach the upper portion of the canvas. The frame is on wheels too and I can lock it in position. I ordered it from an art supply place many years ago and it works like a charm."

Kat was impressed yet again by Simone's independence. It was hard to believe she was the age she was. Age really was just a number.

Katherine looked up and noticed several sets of binoculars on the sill under the row of high windows. There was also a strange headset and some other equipment she did not recognize. None of them had been there on her previous visits. A thought crossed her mind. Were the binoculars for night vision? What could Simone see from up there on her elevated perch?

Simone's eyes had followed hers, and when Kat turned to her, there was a moment of awkwardness before Simone suggested they go to the kitchen. She turned off the music, and they left the studio.

Katherine searched for something to say in a normal voice, as her imagination was racing wildly. "Sometime you must tell me about your passion for Bob Dylan, if that's not too bold to ask."

Simone's expression put her at ease. It also demanded patience.

She is a master at unspoken communication, Kat said to herself.

As if reading her thoughts, Simone sent her another silent message, while she said, "Pas de tout, chérie, not at all. Yes, later I will tell you that, and much more."

They chatted as they sipped tea, speaking mostly about the French health system and Simone's few experiences with it.

"I've lived a remarkably healthy life, so far. But enough about me. Tell me what has been happening in your rêve antibois."

Kat chuckled. Simone had taken to teasing her about her new life in Antibes.

She suspected that Simone knew precisely what Philippe's and her connection was to the events that had just occurred in the cove. However, the subject had not been mentioned since the day Simone had said she didn't know and didn't want to know.

"Living the dream. That's the saying, chérie, non?"

"It often feels that I am. I am loving all the Christmas preparations around the old town—the decorations, the music, the new foods I'm seeing and eating."

Simone smiled, "I haven't seen all that for years but I remember it well. Si beau."

"My big news is that André has chosen five of my photos to hang in his gallery for sale. He's going to enlarge and frame them for me. I'm so excited!"

"That's wonderful! I'm so pleased for you." Simone clapped her hands. "You must bring your portfolio to show me."

Kat had uploaded those five photos and a few others to her phone to show Simone, who praised each of them and also a number of floral shots. They talked about the possibility of Simone painting some of the images one day.

When they parted, Katherine kissed Simone's cheeks extra warmly. She had to resist the urge to hug her, as she had to do with all the French people she especially cared for. It just wasn't done.

"I wish you peace and happiness through the holidays and will be thinking about you."

"Merci, chérie! On the bright side, I don't have to share the delicious cookies and the amazing cheese with anyone. Thank you for your thoughtful gifts. Joyeux Noël en Provence. Call me upon your return."

22

Philippe's daughter, Adorée, flew to Nice from London two days before Christmas. The plan was for her to spend a day at home in Antibes, and then they would all drive up to Joy's for the Christmas Eve feast. It was the first time she had been home since Kat and Philippe had begun living together.

"I'm nervous," Kat said, as they parked on the arrivals level of the airport. "In fact, I'm very nervous."

Philippe patted her hand and reassured her. "Adorée has told us both how happy she is that we are together. You are worrying for nothing."

His words proved true. Adorée was completely relaxed to be around Kat and complimented her several times on the changes to the apartment. "You are making it warm and welcoming again. Finally, we have comfy chairs where we can read. Papa, remember how I always went to my room to lie on my bed when I was reading?"

Philippe tousled her hair. "I'm glad you are happy to be home with us."

"It feels good. I love that you have the crèche set up. You didn't do that for many years."

Philippe lowered his eyes.

Adorée's grateful look spoke volumes to Kat. "He had, what he calls, his dark years. I hope he talks to you about them because he never has with me. Even though I am an adult now, the subject is verboten."

She hugged Kat. "I'm getting used to hugging all the North Americans I work with. I'm so pleased you're making my father happy again."

Philippe's face relaxed as he watched them, but he quickly changed the subject. "Look at the new santons. Change them around as you wish. That used to be your favorite thing to do."

Adorée promptly did just that, exclaiming over her old favorites as well as over the new ones.

That evening they visited several different friends for a glass of champagne. All of them had insisted they bring Adorée along, and Philippe could not stop beaming at having the two women he loved in his life together.

The next day the women did last-minute shopping in the morning. Adorée dashed off with a long list in her hand; Kat had just two stops to make.

She and Philippe had promised they would only exchange small gifts that did not include expensive jewelry. Definitely no rings. They both agreed that Christmas was not the time to decide the future course of their relationship.

As noon approached, they met at the market. While Philippe finished up, Adorée described to Kat the eating that would ensue once they arrived at Joy's.

"Prepare yourself for feasting such as you have never done before," she cautioned. "We used to have two meals, beginning Christmas Eve: one before we all went to la Messe de Minuit and one afterward. Truly a grande fête! But a few years ago everyone agreed it was just too much food. So we have Le Réveillon on Christmas Day now."

Kat had asked Joy how she could contribute to the meals when she had received the invitation, and Joy had responded with her usual thoughtfulness. "It's a main event, my dear. We want you to relax and enjoy it, and there will be plenty of opportunities for you to help, bien sûr. Philippe is responsible for the oysters, fish and cheese. I'm sure he will want your help with that."

After Philippe closed up his stall and loaded the food he was contributing into the car, they went back to the apartment and finished packing. Philippe was exhausted after serving the longest Christmas Eve lines of customers ever and, before they drove off, he handed over the driving duty to Adorée and promptly fell asleep in the back seat as they set off for Sainte Mathilde.

En route, Adorée regaled Kat with tales of Christmas from her childhood, many of them spent at Joy's, as they had alternated the celebrations there with quieter ones at home.

"Sometimes we even went to Paris for Christmas and stayed with Oncle François et Tante Sophie. Sometime you and Papa should spend Christmas in Paris. It's magic. The city feels like a small town with the lights and skating rinks and Christmas markets. C'est magnifique."

By the time they reached the smaller roads leading to Sainte Mathilde, a light snow was falling.

"Oh my! It's almost as if this was ordered," Kat said. "I love having snow on Christmas Eve."

"It was a childhood wish of mine too, from all the American films I watched about Christmas," Adorée said. "One that wasn't often granted."

"It may date me, but Miracle on 34th Street is one of the earliest movies I ever watched. I loved it," Kat said.

Adorée grinned and said that the French version was also a favorite of hers.

The two women liked each other, and a bond was starting to develop between them. Kat appreciated how Adorée appeared to have accepted her as part of her and her father's lives.

The snow was falling heavily now. Colossal, fluffy flakes danced and drifted in the air. The countryside was being transformed into a winter portrait of whites and silvery greys. Long, white rows of trimmed lavender mounds stretched across the fields and vineyards appeared to be draped in sheets, like the furniture in a summer house waiting to be opened and come alive for the season. It was growing dark now, and the dimming light lent its mystery to the winter scene.

Kat reached back to wake Philippe as they turned down the narrow road to the manoir and a few minutes later, she called Joy to say they were turning up the lane. When they arrived Henri was watching for them. He swung open the heavy front door just in time for the three arrivals to burst into the manoir, their arms full of packages.

Most of the extended family had already arrived and were gathered in the grand salon across the bough and bow-laden foyer, singing loudly as Sylvie played a carol on the piano. François was snoozing in a chair by the fire, oblivious to all the activity.

Picasso was the first to reach them, bouncing with excitement and indecision about whom to greet first.

"Ah, Pico! What a beautiful red bow you are sporting." Kat bent down to his level, setting her box of parcels on the floor so she could wrap her arms around him. Her reward was a sloppy Pico kiss on the cheek, making her laugh out loud.

Henri greeted them warmly and helped with the parcels.

As soon as Philippe set down the boxes of seafood and cheese, Antoine and some helpers instantly appeared to carry them off to the kitchen.

One of the young men helped Philippe fetch their suitcases from the car, and soon everything was unloaded and put into the right rooms.

Kat could hear pots and pans being clattered in the kitchen and appetizing aromas wafted down the hall. "I can smell magic happening down there," she exclaimed.

Joy rushed up to greet them, untying a starched white apron and revealing an elegant pairing of a red velvet skirt and a red-and-white silk blouse. She graciously accepted their compliments about her appearance and the scrumptious smell of the meal to come.

"D'accord! Magique, bien sûr! But now you're here we will all pause for some champagne."

Joy flashed Kat a quick look, telegraphing her delight that their problem with Idelle was over. "We have much to celebrate this day!"

With Adorée and Kat on either arm, she walked them around to greet everyone. As well as immediate family, there were cousins and second cousins whom Katherine had not met before. Adorée soon went off with the others her age, while Katherine tried to memorize all the new names.

"Joy, your crèche is fantastique," Kat declared. Set up on a long table against one wall, the display was huge and enthralling. "Of all the crèches I have seen so far, yours is by far the largest and most beautiful. There's a lot of love and family history in it. That's easy to see."

A few people stopped by to pick up their favorite santon and explain its story to her, then Joy put her arm around Katherine and led her to the great hall, which was decorated with boughs and evergreen ropes and a stunning twelve-foot sapin de Noël. The long banquet table in the centre of the room was laid for le grand souper.

"Three white tablecloths, three candles and the three saucers of le blé de Sainte-Barbe all represent the Holy Trinity," Joy explained. "The seven dishes we always serve represent the seven sorrows of the Virgin Mary. Even though we aren't a religious family, at the holidays we still follow the traditions of the church. Did you know we all go to the village church for midnight mass?"

Katherine nodded and said, "I'm honored to be included in all these traditions."

"You're family to us, ma chère."

Back in the salon, Kat searched out François. He was still sitting by the fire, but his snooze was over for now.

"I'm in my usual spot, keeping warm," he said, as she sat down next to him to chat. Katherine was pleased to see he appeared healthy and possibly even a few pounds heavier.

Sylvie walked around the room with a tray of champagne flutes, followed by her daughter and niece with platters of foie gras on toasts.

The children—the girls dressed in flounces of velvet or satin and the boys in dress shirts and trousers—were engrossed in jigsaw puzzles, card games and quiet teasing. There was a lot of giggling.

“Electronics have been banished for the night,” Christian’s wife, Marie, said.

“No one seems to mind,” Kat said.

After some urging, Joy sat down at the piano and the house echoed with song as she played carol after carol as it was requested. Singers wandered in and out of the rooms, sometimes stopping to chat. Kat commented to Adorée how well the youngsters were behaving.

“Oui! Children in France have that reputation,” Adorée said, with a sly grin.

At one point François whispered to Kat and Philippe that he was slipping away for another short nap. “It will be a long evening and I will need my energy for the meal,” he said with a wink.

Offering his arm, Philippe escorted his uncle to his room, promising to come and get him when it was dinnertime.

“You need me for le cacho fio,” François reminded the room as they left.

Katherine was surprised when a group of Joy and Henri’s friends dropped by for a glass of champagne and to exchange greetings. They didn’t stay long, and Henri explained that in recent years their local friends always rented a small bus to take them on the rounds so no one had to drive and the celebrants were back where they were supposed to be for le grand souper.

At eight o’clock, everyone trooped into the great room, and Philippe went up to fetch François. With his silver hair smoothed back and a green cravat tied jauntily around his neck, the old man looked rested and as handsome as Katherine had ever seen him. He was greeted by his rambunctious six-year-old twin great-nephews, who led him to a log lying on the hearth. Together they picked it up and carried it around the table three times. Everyone followed behind.

“C’est le cacho fio, probably from an olive tree,” Henri explained to Kat. “They are the youngest and oldest here and they will sprinkle the log with vin cuit, sweet mulled wine, salt and bread crumbs and light it together while François says the ancient blessing in Provençal.”

Joy sidled in beside Kat and murmured a translation as François and the boys put the log on the fire in the great hall and François blessed it:

"Christmas log
Give us the fire
Let us rejoice
God gives us the joy
Christmas comes, all is well
God give us the favor to see the coming year
And if we are not more
Let us not be less."

The room filled with cries of santé, and everyone moved to the table to look for their name card.

As they ate, her neighbors at the table took it upon themselves to tell Katherine the traditions that were being observed. Adorée told her that the table would stay laid for three days so the angels could have a feast too.

"And the fire burns for three days too," someone else said. "We all make certain of that."

Kat said, "It's hard to believe this was once a simple meal served without any fuss."

"That's right," Joy's son-in-law, Christian, said. "Much has changed through the years but one thing that hasn't is that there's no meat in any of the seven courses."

Some dishes and breads had been set up on a buffet table, including two ornate china tureens, one for an aromatic soup of garlic and herbs and the other for a lightly spiced roasted chestnut soup. Other dishes included escargots, chard stalks in a white sauce, spinach au gratin, celeri à l'anchois, a white bean purée accented with herbes de Provence, and ratatouille. A salted cod dish in a rich red-wine sauce with tomato, olives, and capers, was the highlight of the meal and served with small cross-shaped pasta.

"This is one of maman's specialties, la morue en raito, and we eat it at this meal every year," Sylvie said as she held the platter for Katherine.

"I remember eating cod in le grand aioli for the first time with your family last June on the terrace here. It was delicious."

"And what a lot has happened in your life since then," Joy commented from farther along the table. "That was the day everyone here first met you, and now you are a member of the family."

Seven local wines dotted the tables, and now everyone raised a glass to toast Kat and Philippe. Then Philippe took Kat's hand, and they both rose and thanked everyone for their kind words. Katherine got quite emotional when she talked about how grateful she was for how warmly they had taken her into their family.

Someone said, "Bien, let's eat," and the focus returned to what was on their plates.

With eighteen people around the table and a fire blazing in the hearth, the ambiance was festive and the conversation merry. From time to time, someone would stand and recite a provençal poem or begin a carol, and everyone who knew the words joined in. Katherine was reminded of an oil painting by one of the old masters of just this type of scene. Her heart felt about to burst with gratitude to be included. She was also becoming very full but knew that was the last thing she should say in France.

When the dishes were cleared, Adorée looked at Kat and grinned. "Get ready for it: les treize desserts—the thirteen desserts. They're supposed to symbolize Christ and the twelve apostles, and you must have a bite of each. That's the rule."

Henri stood and, in a ringing voice, announced the arrival of "Les Treize!" The children applauded and cheered.

Katherine was anticipating rich pastries, so she was relieved to see they were quite simple offerings. Philippe and Joy explained their meaning as the dishes were passed around. "Pompe à l'huile is like a brioche, and we must tear it, not cut it; white-and-black nougat, which some say represent Good and Evil; dates, whose oval shape is purportedly the symbol of Christ; the four beggars—dry figs, raisins, almonds and hazelnuts—representing the religious orders of the Franciscans, Dominicans, Carmelites and Augustinians; fresh oranges respresenting wealth in the new year; verdau,- green winter melon preserved on straw; candied citron; dried plums; green and white grapes, which were stored hanging at the back of a cool cellar after les vendanges."

The last dessert to be brought to the table was a large platter of winter pears and apples along with the highlight calissons, the local almond-paste candy from Aix, and pain d'épices, which Katherine called French gingerbread.

After the table was cleared, a final course of coffee and digestifs was served.

François announced he was off to bed. "There was a day when this meal did not exhaust me but that is long gone. Pray for me at la Messe de Minuit, and I will see you in the morning."

Everyone stood to bid him goodnight and the youngest children were rounded up for bed as well, after placing their shoes in front of the fireplace.

"Père Noël will fill them tonight," they assured Katherine, anticipation lighting their eyes. The older children began placing bright paper decorations and wrapped sweets on the sapin de Noël as part of the next morning's surprise.

Some of the men started loading into their cars the boxes of food and clothing they had all brought to donate at the church. Joy suggested to the others that they might like a stroll before la Messe at the church in Sainte Mathilde.

"I've got to walk off some of that meal," Kat said.

"Imagine that we used to come back after mass and start in with Le Réveillon, which is an even bigger meal. Now we save that for tomorrow," Philippe said

"Thank goodness," Katherine murmured. "Thank goodness."

The sound of excited children's laughter woke Kat and Philippe early and they smiled at each other through sleepy eyes. They folded into each other under the cozy duvet, and Philippe whispered, "Joyeux

Noël, Minou. I am so happy to celebrate this special time here with you. You are giving meaning to all these moments for me again."

"Merry Christmas, mon Chou, and Joyeux Noël. You know I feel the same. Happiness is the gift you continue to give me."

Kissing, they lay comfortably in an embrace. Philippe lightly ran his fingers across her belly and down. Kat closed her eyes and moaned softly.

They had drifted back to sleep when a light tap on the door and a cheery voice told them that a breakfast buffet would soon be served.

Kat emerged from the en suite shower to discover an envelope taped to the mirror, with her name on it in Philippe's distinctive handwriting.

"What's this?" she asked, taking it into the bedroom.

"It's just a little extra something," Philippe said with a wide grin.

Kat opened the envelope and took out a photo of a young puppy, bright-eyed and fluffy, that looked like pictures she had seen of the young Picasso. "Is it Pico as a pup?"

"No. It's your new pup."

Kat looked at him, excited and confused. "Whaaa ...?"

"Well, it represents your new pup, I should say. A litter was born a few weeks ago, at Picasso's breeder, and one pup is reserved for you. We will go at the end of January so you can pick him or her out yourself."

Kat leapt on Philippe and they both fell back on the bed. "I can't believe it! What an amazing surprise. You weren't supposed to give me a big gift for Christmas."

"I couldn't resist. This is for all the love and patience you have shown in dealing with my problem. I couldn't think of anything you would like more."

Kat sat on the bed and cried. Happy tears covered her face for several minutes before she was able to speak. Each time she attempted to say something, more tears appeared. When she looked at the adorable pup in the photo, more tears appeared. Philippe sat beside her, handing her tissues, his throat tight with emotion and his eyes sparkling at her reaction, damp as it was.

"This is so wonderful," she finally managed to say. "So absolutely wonderful—and so sweet of you. How exciting! We will pick him out together. I can't wait."

She bounced around the room and hugged him several more times, as he reveled in her joy.

Her excitement echoed throughout the house as Kat shared the surprise of Philippe's gift with everyone, including Pico.

The rest of the morning passed quietly. Kat decided everyone was still recovering from the exuberance of the night before and resting in preparation for what was to come. The adults exchanged small, thoughtful gifts while the children unwrapped new toys and games.

"Our family has always exchanged gifts on New Year's Day," Joy told Kat. "Christmas is more about family and food and less about gift-giving. Still, we give the children something small they can play with."

François invited Katherine to a game of bridge with two others at a table set by the fire in the library. Children were settled in various places working on puzzles, reading or making up their own games. Philippe and Joy sat together in a quiet corner of the room, chatting and laughing as they enjoyed the scene unfolding around them.

"Life as it should be," Joy commented, while a relieved Philippe admitted he had wondered for a while in the previous month if that would ever happen.

The aromas floating down the hall from the kitchen had most of the group salivating by the time the dinner bell was rung, and Le Réveillon started at 1:00 p.m. The atmosphere in the house livened immediately.

The feast began with smoked salmon, followed by oysters, assorted filets of fish in a variety of sauces; baked fish; and, brought it with great fanfare and majestically presented, lobster, crab legs, shrimp and the family's favorite scallop dish, Coquilles Saint-Jacques.

"You warned me this was a decadent, luxurious meal, and you were right," Kat whispered to Adorée.

Turkey stuffed with chestnuts and beef tournedos topped with foie gras were the main courses, accompanied by classic Lyonnaise potatoes and roasted root vegetables.

Katherine soon realized that the extended meal was a splendid example of the art of having a meaningful conversation while savoring fine food. Whether it was simply a fresh baguette and cheese or a feast, food in France was always savored and discussed, not simply eaten.

After the dishes were cleared and small dessert plates passed around, a fresh fruit platter arrived along with trays of the cheeses that Philippe had brought. There were exclamations of appreciation around the table and more than one person rose to toast the entire meal.

In due course, Henri sounded a trumpet-like fanfare while the others stood and rhythmically clapped. Hélène and Antoine appeared, with beaming smiles, carrying between them a long board with what looked to Katherine like a large chocolate-covered cake roll.

The children squealed, "La bûche de Noël!"

"The Christmas Yule Log," Philippe explained. "The lightest, most delicious vanilla Genoise sponge cake with the richest homemade chocolate buttercream glaçage. I have never tasted one better than the one baked in this kitchen."

Adorée leaned in and added, "You can't possibly resist this, Kat. See how the children have decorated it with holly and mushrooms. The mushrooms aren't real, although they look it. They're made from meringue. Only the holly is real. I was in the kitchen helping with it."

Not one serving was refused.

Later in the afternoon, tired and happy, people began leaving for home. Adorée had asked if they could get back to Antibes that evening so that she could spend the next day with friends before returning to London on December 27.

"This has been wonderful," Kat said to Joy as they hugged. "I am always so happy to have a chance to really hug someone when I am with you. Thank goodness you did not give up that part of your English heritage."

Joy laughed. "It's one of the many reasons I am always thrilled to see you too. Thank you for sharing this holiday with us and making it even more special."

"It was an incredible experience, Joy. I thank you—and all the family—for making me so welcome. I loved the traditions and the camaraderie—and the food. Oh, the food!"

They hugged again and Joy whispered into her ear, "Philippe has assured me the problems have all been resolved. I am so happy for you both."

Kat's smile lit up her face. "It is such a relief. Everything seemed to happen very quickly, and now we can get on with our plans for the future."

François was next in line. He kissed her hand and held it between his while he told her what pleasure it had given him to have her there. "And your bridge playing is magnifique!"

When she protested, he shushed her and made her promise to return soon so he could arrange another game.

Philippe and Adorée took just as long to say their goodbyes, but finally they all settled into the car and headed south.

23

Adorée returned to London on the 27th. Their goodbyes were quite emotional.

"This was the best Christmas since Maman passed away," she said, her voice almost steady. "It felt like I truly was home again."

Philippe stumbled in his response, and his daughter put her arms around him.

"Papa, you forget I am all grown up now. Time has passed, and it makes me happy to see you finally move on with your life."

Turning to Kat, she held her hand with both of hers. "Kat, you are just the woman I hoped Papa would find."

Kat would have liked to hug her, but restrained herself to a bise and thanked her for making the holiday complete. "Come home again soon."

Later, as they sat reading in the salon, Kat looked up from her book. "The apartment feels empty without her. It was so lovely to have her with us."

"C'est vrai." Philippe said. "It felt right, and thanks in no small part to you."

"It was a happy time," Kat agreed, then she sneezed loudly. "After all the rich food we ate this week, shall I make us poached eggs on toast for dinner?"

"Yes, please. I feel the need for comfort food too—with no wine!" Philippe said. "And an early bedtime. I have a big order arriving before dawn tomorrow."

Kat woke early the next morning, with cold shivers, a fever and stuffed sinuses.

"I thought you were Superwoman," Philippe teased. "I will pick up some medicines on my way home and you are to stay in bed. It's very early so try to go back to sleep."

It turned out to be a nasty flu bug, and by the next day Philippe had fallen victim to it as well. For the first time in a long while he took two days away from the market because of illness.

"It's been years," he told her. "Thank goodness for Gilles."

For that time they stayed buried under their duvet, reading, sleeping and talking excitedly about their new pup.

"I can't wait until the end of the month," Kat pretended to moan. "Can't we get him now?" Philippe proposed they each make a list of names to see if they included a match.

"But, you know, Minou, we won't be able to decide until we see him. He will let us know which of these names should be his."

"It sounds like we've decided it will be a male. Like our Pico. I'm going to circle a date on our calendar right now and begin a countdown!"

Between conversations and naps, they took turns making lemon tea with honey. On la Saint-Sylvestre, New Year's Eve day, they started to feel close to normal again. Philippe returned to the stall, and Kat joined him in the afternoon to help set up the market hall for the traditional feast and soirée dansante. Space was cleared for dancing and dining, heaters were set up and le gui, mistletoe, was hung.

"At least we don't have to get up too early tomorrow for the bain du jour de l'an at the beach in Salis."

"A New Year's day swim? In the Med? Are you serious?"

"Oui. Don't worry, we don't take the plunge until 11:30. It's a tradition for all of us to have this dip in La Grande Bleue on the first day of the new year."

Kat looked at him in shock until she caught the twinkle in his eye.

"Ha! Let's just try to make the fireworks tomorrow evening at the beach in Juan-les-Pins," she said, and they agreed that might well be something they could manage.

Late in the afternoon, they decided to take a nap before heading out to the festivities, and Philippe wakened to his cellphone ringing at 11:15 p.m. André was calling to see why they had not shown up yet.

Philippe looked over at Kat, who was snoring lightly in a way he found quite sweet, and thought about waking her. Then he reconsidered and told André they would be staying home. He soon fell back to sleep himself.

When they woke up early the next morning, they shared a laugh at how their first New Year's Eve had not turned out as planned

"C'est la vie, mon amour. I'm glad you didn't wake me up." Kat said as they wished each other bon jour de l'an with a long list of good things they hoped for, each item followed by a kiss.

"Let's take our time this morning and then go watch the crazy nageurs at the beach. I told André we would meet them there."

They spent much of the day hanging out with friends, first at Salis beach, then at lunch at a nearby bistro known for its delicious croque monsieurs. Kat had developed a serious liking for the toasted ham sandwich with Emmental cheese grilled on top.

In the afternoon, they phoned Andrea and Terrence to give them their best wishes for the new year.

"Happy New Year to you too, darling Kat and Philippe. We're sorry the kids are all out doing their own thing, but we will pass along your good wishes. We miss you."

Next they called Molly, who sounded very happy and not alone, although she admitted nothing. "We hope this is a wonderful year for you, Moll, in every way. A new beginning."

"And for you two lovebirds as well," Molly said. "I miss you, Katski. We have to make some plans. Bring Philippe to Toronto for a visit."

"You never know," Philippe said. "I would like to do that."

When they hung up, Kat and Philippe commented at the same time that Molly had not dropped one f-bomb during the conversation.

"That counseling is really working."

"Maybe she made it a New Year's resolution too."

After dark that evening they met Annette and her husband, along with Gilles and his cousins who were visiting, and a few others friends on the beach in Juan-les-Pin for the fireworks display.

"Every time we watch fireworks, I think I will never see a more spectacular display and the next time they simply outdo the show," Kat remarked, as they climbed into bed.

Philippe agreed and held Kate tightly. "Thank you for making the holidays so much fun and full of meaning again. You even made getting the flu feel special."

Kat missed seeing Simone. They had last talked on la Saint-Sylvestre, when Kat called to wish her well and explain that she would come to see her when she was over the flu.

"The last thing I want to do is expose you to this nasty germ, Simone. You would not thank me for that."

Simone's response was quick and sure. "Getting sick last month was all the illness I needed for a very long time."

Then she surprised Katherine by saying she would be having some company for a few days.

"Every year at the first of January, an art dealer from Paris and his wife come to visit and do business. They are old friends of Jean-Luc's and getting on themselves but he is well established and still very active. I will tell you all about it when I see you next. They will stay until Epiphany so come after that, chérie."

24

January 6th was the celebration of Epiphany.

"I should have known this would involve eating in some way," Kat laughed as Philippe presented her with a galette des rois after dinner, a lightly sugared brioche topped with a paper crown. He cut it into three slices and Kat bit into one. Then she winced and sputtered, and spat out a porcelain bean into a tissue.

"What is it?" Kat asked. "It almost broke my tooth!"

Philippe was apologetic. "Oh là là—I forgot to warn you. Sorry! You got la fève. There's only one in the cake, and finding it brings you good luck."

Kat shot him a look as she rinsed the charm at the sink.

Philippe placed the paper crown on her head. "You are now king for the day and your first wish will be granted."

"My wish has already been granted," Kat said. "The Idelle situation has been resolved. Nothing stands in the way of our plans for the property on the Cap now. I am so excited. This project and our new pup are going to make this a banner year."

Each day was again bringing Kat affirmation that this was the life and the love she was meant to have.

Yesterday, Philippe had brought home his architect's plans for the renovations to the villa on the Cap. They had spread them on the dining table that night and pored over every detail, making notes about changes they wanted to see. Philippe went out of his way to let Kat know this was a joint project and that her opinions and ideas were as important as his.

Now they took the drawings out again and talked some more about their hopes and dreams. Laughing as they, not too seriously, considered what they might name the inn, they decided to go to the property the next day and walk through, plans in hand.

"The new life we're building together begins once again with these plans. That is a promise, Minou."

Kat ran her hands lightly over the blueprints. She thought she might never have felt happier than this moment. "This is our future."

"The work is going to begin the week after next if we want it to," Philippe continued. "When I spoke to the contractor, Didier, last October, he had scheduled the job to begin around the first week of January. After all the trouble began with Idelle, I never cancelled it. I just didn't think of it. So we have not lost any time. What do you think, Kat? Shall we go ahead with it?"

Nodding her head and grinning, no words were necessary.

"It's amazing how things work out because, when I met with him yesterday, Didier told me that if we could not begin right away he would have to put it off for a year. He has been offered a big job in Juan-les-Pins, but he said he would honor his commitment to us first."

"We have a year, at least, to think about it before we welcome our first guest. You know the way it goes with contractors and restoration work. It may take even longer."

Kat looked at Philippe, her heart full. "We have such an exciting future ahead of us, I don't care how long it takes. The important thing is that we are doing what you promised me months ago. How could the start of this new year be any better?"

The galette des rois sat forgotten on the table.

Her cellphone rang just after 10:30 that night. Katherine assumed it was either Andrea or Molly preparing to Skype.

"Hey there. Bonne soirée here. Bon après-midi to you," she answered.

"Kat? It's Terrence. Oh God, Kat ... there's been a terrible accident."

"Is Andrea all right?" she gasped. "The kids? What happened?"

"It's Molly, and the news is not good."

"No!"

Her shout brought Philippe to her side, and he put his arm around her shoulder.

"The roads are very icy from a storm last night," Terrence said. "Instead of coming for lunch, Molly decided to change her plans and meet Andrea at an auction and then join us for dinner. They were on their way here, in their own cars, when hers was hit head on. She's in a coma. Andrea is okay. She was just ahead of Molly and heard the crash. She's at the hospital with her now."

Katherine wiped away tears, her voice catching as she asked questions, some that could not be answered.

"It happened a few miles from here—you know that sharp corner by the old sawmill."

"What can I do? I'll come right away. This is terrible ..." and with that she broke down and passed the phone to Philippe.

He and Terrence spoke for a few more minutes before hanging up.

Philippe held her close and stroked her hair, trying his best to comfort her, as she sobbed uncontrollably.

"She can't ... She can't ... die. She just can't ..."

"Don't give up hope. Terrence says they have few details but Andrea stressed Molly is not on life support and is holding her own. He will call later, or Andrea will, as soon as they have more to tell us."

Kat sat in a daze for a long time, unable to go to bed, then she got up and started pacing, focusing every positive thought on Molly, willing her to recover. Philippe went online to look into flights to Toronto and texted to let Gilles know he would not be at the market the next day. Gilles texted back not to worry as the market would be quiet, with everyone still recovering from the holidays.

Kat was beside herself, muttering repeatedly. "I can't believe this! How could this happen to Molly? After all she's been through in her life. How is it possible?"

Around midnight, Andrea called to report that Molly was being kept in a medically induced coma to help reduce the pressure in her brain.

"I'm so sorry, Kat. I know how terrible you must be feeling. We all are ..." Her voice faltered and she stopped speaking for a moment. "Father DeCarlo is here and bringing us all what comfort he can."

Hearing that he was there reassured Katherine. No one knows Molly better, she told Philippe.

Andrea continued. "He told me that when he was in Vancouver with Molly after Shawn died, he helped her draw up a living will and a Power of Attorney for both property and personal care. The person she named is you."

"Oh my gosh, that's right. I remember her asking me if that was all right."

"It means it would be best if you could be here, as soon as you can manage. There are papers that require your signature. There will be decisions to make. The hospital will scan and email some forms to you immediately, but they say you really should be here. I'm sure you want to be. I don't know what else to say. I can't think clearly."

Fear for her friend clouded Kat's mind, and she passed the phone to Philippe once more, so he could listen to the instructions.

After he hung up, Kat looked at him, her eyes filled with pain. "I have to go, no question."

"We will both go. I will make the reservations now."

Kat sat, stunned, before her thoughts began to unjumble.

"It doesn't make any sense for you to come right now. We don't know how long Molly will be like this. I'll get an open ticket. Besides, you have to be here to get work started on the villa. And for the market."

"I guess that makes sense, but it doesn't feel right," said Philippe, hesitating, his voice tight. "But you must go to be with Molly and to take care of any decisions. I promise to be with you as soon as I can or as soon as you say."

Kat gulped back tears, drawing strength from his calm support.

"What matters now is Molly, Kat. You are the most important person she has in her life. I know that. She needs you. Let's call the airline now."

"I know, I know. I want to be there with her. I need to … I just can't believe this is happening."

All flights to Toronto were full for the next day but the day after was fine, although she would have to wait three hours in Paris between flights. Philippe made a decision and booked two flights to Paris the next day and then one for Kat to Toronto the day after.

"At least I can do the Paris part of the trip with you and we will have a quiet evening there. Then I'll see you off on your flight to Toronto. That will be less tiring for you too."

They both knew they would not fall asleep for a while. Kat warmed some mugs of milk, hoping that would help, and they phoned Terrence with the flight information.

"We'll call you tomorrow as soon as we know what is happening," he said, "and I'll meet you at the airport. She may be transferred to a Toronto hospital but that decision hasn't been made yet."

They sat at the kitchen table in silence for a while, sipping the milk.

"The unpredictability of life …" Philippe muttered. "We thought we had problems but they were nothing compared to this."

"Promise me we will talk at least once a day."

"Probably more, mon amour. We have to deal with it moment by moment and trust all will be well. We have to do everything we can to help Molly get better."

Resting her head on Philippe's shoulder, Kat wept quietly. She could feel the love and concern in his embrace and she took comfort from the strength of his body pressed to hers.

"Molly has to get better. She just has to. I need her in our life."

"Molly will be part of our life for a very long time to come. The rest is unimportant. We must believe that."

"We must …" Kat was sobbing again, as much as she tried to stop.

Rocking her gently, he continued. "And you will be back here in my arms before we know it. We have a life to live together."

"Yes, we do," she stammered through her tears. "And promises to keep."

"Oui, Minou … my sweet Kat. Sans aucun doute. Of that there is no doubt. "

A Note to My Readers

Thank you for reading *Promises To Keep.*

When I finished writing *The Promise of Provence,* I thought that Katherine's story had ended. (I loved writing it, by the way!)

But then your emails began arriving—by the hundreds and then thousands—asking what happens next. I was touched that so many of you cared about Katherine and Philippe and the other characters so much you wanted more!

I thought I would write a short follow-up story, describing the life Katherine and Philippe began after they walked out of the airport together. But that was not to be.

As I wrote, I began to discover more about the characters, and the story became increasingly complicated. New characters appeared, and it was as if Kat and Philippe took hold of the story and carried me along.

I also learned from your responses that you share my love for the south of France. That particular part of the world, with its beauty, culture and history, has become a character in its own right.

As a result, I'm going to continue writing about Katherine and Philippe and the south of France, as well as Molly and Andrea and Terrence and Joy and Adorée and François and all the others you first met in *The Promise of Provence.* Now Simone, Véronique and David as well as Annette and Gilles have joined the cast. I think you will be happy to get to know even more intriguing characters making their way into the narrative.

I'm excited to keep writing about them all, and I'm full of ideas for what happens next. I sometimes feel I'm simply a bystander who has been invited along on their adventure. The stories will continue until they, or you, let me know they are over.

What do you think? Have I made a good decision? I value your thoughts and opinions, so please share them with me right here: patriciasandsauthor@gmail.com

Have you signed up for my newsletter? It goes out once a month with all sorts of contests and information about what's coming next. The subscription link can be found at my website: patriciasandsauthor.com

If you have time to write a brief review I would be most grateful. Comments from readers are so helpful and inspiring. You are the reason I write and your words encourage others to read my books.

I want to express my sincere thanks to my family and friends for their ongoing support and to my editor, Dinah Forbes, for her wisdom and guidance. I owe a big bouquet of gratitude in particular to Magali Prince and Ida Young-Bondi for their valued guidance with all things French. Thanks also to my advance readers who offer me honest, helpful comments and lots of laughter! I can never repay my brother, Terry Murphy, a writer of non-fiction and highly praised educational texts as well as a voracious reader, for his priceless assistance, opinions, and superb proofreading skills … and he keeps reminding me of this! Thanks to Amy Cooper and Barb Drozdowich (my tech angel!) for their dedication and active involvement in all I do. Kudos to Scott Collie and Carrie Spencer for another fabulous cover!

And now … on to the next book!

About the Author

PATRICIA SANDS lives in Toronto, Canada, when she isn't somewhere else. An admitted travel fanatic, she can pack a bag in a flash and be ready to go anywhere … particularly the south of France. With a focus on travel, women's issues and ageing, her stories celebrate the feminine spirit and the power of friendship. Encouraging women of all ages to stare down the fear factor and embrace change, Patricia has heard from readers (men too!) ages 20 to 83.

Her award-winning debut novel *The Bridge Club* was published in 2010 and her second novel, *The Promise of Provence* recently received a 2014 National Indie Excellence Finalist Award in Literary Fiction. An Amazon Hot New Release in April 2013, *The Promise of Provence* was also a USA Best Book 2013 Finalist. Patricia returned to France in September 2013 for a book signing, hosted by Heidi's English Bookshop in Antibes, and also spent a month researching her next novel, *Promises To Keep.*

Thanks to reader requests, these two novels set in the south of France are now the beginning of the *Love In Provence* series. *Promises To Keep — Love In Provence,* Book Two, is available on Amazon, iTunes, B&N, and Kobo.

The audiobook of *The Bridge Club* should be available at the end of 2014.

In June 2014, Patricia led two 10-day tours of the French Riviera and the countryside of Provence. These trips were based on *The Promise of Provence,* with the WOMEN'S TRAVEL NETWORK (womenstravelnetwork.ca/promenade-en-provence). Let her know if you would like to go in 2015! She is already counting the days to her return.

Find out more at:

Patricia's Facebook Author Page: facebook.com/AuthorPatriciaSands
Amazon Author Page: www.amazon.com/Patricia-Sands/e/B004CSUD2Q/
Goodreads: www.goodreads.com/patriciasands

Or her blog where you will find links to her books, social media, and monthly newsletter. The latter, sent once a month, contains special giveaways as well as her photography and information about the south of France, her home away from home. She would love to hear from you!

Patricia can also be found:
twitter.com/patricia_sands
patriciasandsauthor.com

ALSO BY PATRICIA SANDS

(NOW ALSO AVAILABLE AS AN AUDIOBOOK)

THE BRIDGE CLUB

Eight women. Four Decades.
One unimaginable weekend.
How far would you go to help a good friend?
Is there a place where you might draw the line?

Where can you find a story about friendship, laughter and the good things in life that also touches on alcoholism, infidelity, porn addiction, terminal illness and grief? For most women, it's often within their own circle of friends.

Author Patricia Sands reminds us of the complexities of womens friendships in her new book, *The Bridge Club*, a moving tale of eight women whose lives intersect once a month initially to play the game of bridge. What began as one night turns into four decades that span the segments of a woman's journey from youthful optimism to embracing the challenges and opportunities presented in life's later years.

Based loosely on her own bridge club, Sands weaves the reader through a maze of life's inevitable scenarios as the club bears the death of a member's spouse, one woman's meeting with her biological mother, the inevitable marital and health issues, and another's final chance at freedom through the most difficult choice.

"There are many subjects I address in the book that are controversial. Some people may wonder if they were chosen to thicken the plot," says Sands. "Although I have taken liberties with the actual events, and it is truly a work of fiction, most issues faced by the characters in the book were experienced in my own bridge club. The bottom line of the story is a testament to friendship and hope."

The final chapter of *The Bridge Club* challenges our principles as one woman begins to descend into dementia.

Awards

Foreword Reviews **2010 Book of the Year – General Fiction**

2011 Next Generation Indie Book Awards
(First Novel – over 80,000 words)

2012 Indie Excellence Book Awards – Womens Fiction

Reviews of *The Bridge Club*

"Reading Patricia Sand's *The Bridge Club* feels a little like taking a long road trip with a friend, she drives as we listen to her narrate this story of eight female characters, a condensed version of their lives, her voice like the gentle thrum of the engine, lulling us at times into a companionable silence, we listen and observe the passing landscape of years, immersing into these lives as if they were our own." — Claire McAlpine (Amazon)

"This was a wonderful book. *The Bridge Club*, a novel by Patricia Sands, is one of those books that you treasure while you're reading it and can't wait to share with friends. The lovely story of a forty year friendship among eight women is beautifully written and touches the heart. The problems these women face over the years cover so many issues that women of today are dealing with. Lots of laughs, lots of tears and a book to be remembered long after the ending is reached." — Karla Darcy (Goodreads)

THE PROMISE OF PROVENCE
Love In Provence – Book 1

June in Provence is full of promise when Katherine arrives from Canada, eager to feel renewed by her surroundings.

lEndless rows of lavender prepare to burst into pink and purple blooms. Fields of sunflowers flow in golden waves among vineyards and olive groves overlooked by ancient hilltop villages. It's the postcard setting she envisioned, but is that all she needs?

After a year of heartbreak, Katherine has impulsively agreed to a home exchange in the south of France. Colorful locals, a yellow lab named Picasso, and the inspiring beauty of the countryside breathe new life into her days.

Seeking to shed the pain of betrayal and loss, she struggles to recapture her joie de vivre and searches for the answer to a haunting question: is it too late to begin again?

" Be prepared to fall in love with Provence! This is a story that will draw you in with its vibrancy in setting and characters. A must read for any woman with a desire for romance and travel." —Steena Holmes, author of Amazon bestseller *Finding Emma*

Awards

2013 USA Best Book Award ~ Finalist, Chick/Women's Lit

2014 National Indie Excellence Award ~ Finalist, Literary Fiction

Reviews of *The Promise of Provence*

"I am left with a feeling of joy, contentment and happiness as each chapter of this book warmed my heart. A book of life, the challenges and rewards that follow, the characters became special to me and I yearn to read more of them." — Sweettalk (Amazon)

"One has to love a book that touches every emotion! I cried, I laughed and I got lost in all the descriptive Locations and felt like I was reading my own story. A great read!"

— Jayne (Amazon)

38658626R00121

Made in the USA
Lexington, KY
19 January 2015